Destiny's Mission

a novel

Joanne Simon Tailele

Simon Publishing LLC

Joanne Simon Tailele

Paperback ISBN: 978-1-7376246-4-6
eBook ISBN: 979-8-9861221-9-9

Library of Congress Control Number: 2023905647

Published by Simon Publishing LLC
Naples, Florida
United States of America

www.simonpublishingllc.com

With all my love, this book is dedicated to my daughter, Candeus Anne Cooper

Special thanks to my dear friends at Marco Island Writers Inc. for the support and friendship we have shared over the years. Special thanks go to Jennie Weckelman and Pauline Hayton as well as beta readers, T. Milton Mayer and Pamela Raleigh.
Additional thanks must go to my fabulous editor, Suanne Shafer and cover designer, Robin Ludwig with R.L. Designs.

Destiny's Mission

One

A *new normal*—the term the Office of Personnel Management used when Destiny had processed out of the Army after serving her country for twelve years. Stone-faced, she stared at the officer as he handed her the DD-214, Certificate of Release or Discharge from Active Duty. Destiny slipped the paper into her rucksack and then stared out into the abyss. What was normal, anyhow? What did he know? All his chest candy didn't mean a damn thing. As a lifer with two good arms and hands, he hadn't a clue about her normal. After twelve years of service, she received eight hours of propaganda about VA benefits, a "thanks for your service," and then sent on her way. Come on. How about some guidance on how to survive out there with one arm? She felt neither happy nor sad. Strange was a better description. She'd been military her whole life; first as a military brat, a year at USMAPS (United States Military Academy Preparatory School), a four-year West Point grad with a major in International Affairs, then finally a soldier and an officer in the United States Army. Her career had been a long haul, but thanks to her colonel father and Senator Morgan from North Carolina, she'd made it.

Who was she as a civilian? Once off the base and out of her uniform, Destiny felt like she'd been transported to a new planet. She ate alone, shopped alone, lived alone. The server at the local diner always greeted her with a smile and a "table for one?" Some days, Destiny wanted to slap the smile right off the server's face and say, "No, a party of five." But there was no party of five. Instead, Destiny nodded and followed the server to the small single table back by the kitchen. Who wanted to watch an amputee eat alone?

It had been a long haul. After the blast, Destiny hadn't been sure she wanted to live, let alone paint, which had always been her solace. The fact she still had her good right arm seemed of little consequence. Through the first six months, she endured more surgeries than she could count. When she met Sergeant Lakeisha Abraham at Walter Reed, things began to change. Lakeisha lost both her arms at the shoulder, but her optimism was contagious. Lakeisha wrote sexy romance novels with a voice-activated computer and planned to run in the Special Olympics someday. "Hey, Captain," she said every morning in the physical therapy rooms. "What's your gripe? You still got one good arm. Stop your bellyaching. Pick up that brush. Life could be way worse."

Destiny didn't want to hear it. While she had taken minor courses at West Point to become an accredited art therapist, she never dreamed her efforts would be for herself. She'd received the degree and was awaiting accreditation before she left for Afghanistan. Now, she only cared about wallowing in her injury and mourning Max's death. She should have saved him. He was under her command.

But Lakeisha didn't give up. Her 'glass half full' view finally encouraged Destiny to pick up a brush again. Slowly, ever so damn slowly. Whatever talent she'd had dried up. She'd hold a brush in her hand, and forgetting for a second, she'd reach toward the palette that should have been in her left hand. But there was no left hand. The palette sat flat on the table beside her.

It took more than a day or a week or a month. But finally, things began to change. The sun shone a little brighter. She began to really paint. The grotesque paintings of twisted, broken bodies slowly evolved into something she never dreamed she'd see: the smiling faces of hopeful amputees. Before she left Walter Reed, her physical therapist noticed the miraculous change in Destiny's painting and encouraged her to consider teaching art.

She had no idea what to do with herself outside of the Army. Should she look for a job? Doing what? She was a good negotiator with third-world leaders, but how would that help her on American soil?

Habit still had her rising at 4:30 a.m. every morning. Civilian life certainly afforded more sleep time, even if her internal clock disagreed. The first morning she slept until six felt like another victory.

Simple things frustrated her most. Did anyone realize how hard it was to pull up your pants with one hand? Humans were meant to have two arms, two legs, two hands, two feet. This wasn't natural. Driving a car, Destiny used to hold the steering wheel with her left hand when she shifted gears with her right. Not anymore. It helped a little when she traded in her beloved little standard transmission Mustang for a nondescript automatic transmission sedan.

Before leaving Walter Reed, she received her new hand. It was twice the size of her normal hand. "My God," she said. "What the hell is this thing?"

They secured it to her stump and explained how her brain would send signals to the prosthetic. She tried to concentrate. *Move, you damn thing.* Nothing. Not even a finger moved.

"It's not going to happen overnight," said the prosthetic technician. "It's a very sophisticated device. It will learn your signals. When you contract your upper arm, it sends signals down to the device. Think of it as a computer learning your actions. Repetition will make it work."

"Does it have to be this ugly to work?"

The tech chuckled. "Sorry. We haven't designed a smaller version yet. Most of our patients are—"

"Men." Destiny finished his sentence.

"Er, yes." The young man dipped his head, and a blush crept up his neck to his cheeks. "We haven't had a big demand for female prosthetics."

"I guess that's a good thing," replied Destiny.

Two weeks later, Destiny was able to flex the fingers and pick up most things. It hadn't been an easy two weeks. No one saw the days she cried into her pillow or threw things against the wall. On days like that, she was glad she was alone so no one witnessed her melt downs.

The MD at Walter Reed encouraged her to finish her degree in Art Therapy. With a few phone calls, she had a Zoom interview with Master Sergeant Clemmons at Fort Jackson, North Carolina, for an art therapist position on the base with the Wounded Warrior project. He liked the fact that she was a disabled vet and thought she would relate well with the other soldiers. It was a volunteer position. Some day she would need to get a paying job, but for now, it was the exact transition she needed. She breathed a sigh of relief that she could still be a part of the military community after she gained civilian status.

With her VA benefits, she purchased a little bungalow in Columbia, South Carolina, a quick thirty-minute drive across the state line from Fort Jackson. A sense of pride filled her heart when the real estate agent pulled the *Sale Pending* sign from the yard and handed over the keys. Destiny glanced down, and her eyes lingered on the triangular frame she clutched tightly to her chest. It held a United States Flag, a parting gift from the Army. She knew exactly where it would go: in a place of honor above the fireplace.

A week later, she'd moved in. The new-to-her furniture, sparse as it was, sat finally in place. After fingering the chintz curtains, she ran her bare feet over the handmade hooked rug and plopped into the overstuffed sofa. A smile spread across her lips. All a far cry from military issue, but it felt good. Feminine. For the first time in years, she let her chestnut hair touch her collar. Her body—minus one forearm and hand—was still fit, and she had all her faculties. Well, most of them. This was her new normal.

In the tiny bedroom, Destiny struggled into a pair of jeans and a long-sleeve white shirt that covered the prosthetic arm and part of her bionic-man hand. She grabbed her sketch pads and charcoals and headed for the base. If she dawdled anymore, she'd be late for her appointment. Soldiers from the Wounded Warrior project at Fort Jackson counted on her to help them through their own transition.

Outside, she paused again to look at the tiny bungalow. The miniscule yard leading to the front door was trimmed neatly. Matching terracotta pots filled with bright pink and white impatiens graced either side of the front stoop. An American flag waved from one pot and the Army flag from the other. A smile crossed her lips. She was home, really home.

She turned the key in the ignition of her rickety old sedan and headed east toward Fort Jackson.

At the base, Private First-Class Teddy Roosevelt waited in the art room of the rehab facility. As she entered, he gave a curt nod, not looking in the least happy about his therapy.

"Hey, grunt. Why the long face?" Destiny smiled as she chided him.

He shoved the tray of charcoal pencils with his stump, watching them crash to the floor. "This is a fuckin' waste of time. How do I get out of this shit?"

Destiny bent to pick them up. "Once you show some effort. Sergeant Collins said you were a doodler, that you made cartoon sketches on everything in the barracks. That talent is still in there. We simply need to pull it out."

"*Ppft*. That was when I had a hand to draw with. What am I going to do with this?" He held up the stump of his right forearm.

"You still have your left hand, private, and once you get your prosthetic, you may be able to draw with that stump, too." She flexed the fingers on her prosthetic hand. "Don't be so quick to give up." Destiny set the pencils back in front of him and rearranged the easel and canvas. "You're pissed off about what happened over there. I get it. I'm pissed too. But that's not going to change anything. Put that anger on the canvas. Show me." She lifted a charcoal pencil and placed it in his left hand.

Teddy grasped the pencil with his left hand and glared at it. He made one swipe across the canvas. Then another. And another. The image of an Afghan soldier began to emerge. Before long, he was engrossed in what he was doing.

The sketch was rough and the lines jagged, but Destiny could clearly see his intent. She silently set up her own easel beside him and began to draw Teddy's profile: his wide nose, deep set black eyes, tense jaw, fixed tight in concentration, or —more than likely—anger.

Her second appointment, Master Sergeant Allen Crow was making tremendous progress. A double amputee at the knees, he came to her while still on a suicide watch. Across his left hand, the letters L I F E were tattooed. He said it was to remind him every day to choose life. Today he was finishing up a charcoal sketch of his hand, the letters prominent across his knuckles. The drawing said it all.

That evening, in the comfort of her little bungalow, Destiny reflected on Teddy, Allen, and the dozens of other soldiers that came to her for therapy. Some were more willing than others to try. Some had real talent, like Teddy. Others, like Allen, started out with stick figures drawn by a five-year-old, but the effort the drawings required gave them something to think about other than their disabilities. Destiny's heart filled with joy that she could contribute something to these men and women. They were all scarred, inside and out. The suicide rate among wounded veterans was staggering. If she could keep even one from giving up on life, all her efforts were worth it. Five days a week, she would give her best to reach them. And maybe, some of her scars would heal as well.

The next morning, she'd made it to the end of the driveway when a taxi pulled up to the curb, blocking her in. She slammed on the brakes, so she didn't crash into it. The taxi had barely stopped when out stepped her little sister, Angela, wearing her usual three-inch spectator pumps, and skinny jeans. But her normally perfect coif and impeccable make-up were noticeably missing. She stopped and waved but didn't smile.

Angela? What on earth was she doing there? Throwing the car in park and turning off the engine, Destiny jumped out. Her sister looked like hell. Something was wrong. Dropping by without notice? That was not like her at all.

Angela dropped her Prada bags and ran toward her sister, arms splayed to wrap her in a hug. She stopped dead in her tracks as her gaze traveled to Destiny's left side. The long sleeve covered Destiny's left arm, but the man-hand stopped her cold. Angela's face crumpled. "Um ... Dezi?"

Destiny tucked the prosthetic behind her back. She could always tell when it made people nervous. "It's okay, Angela. I'm fine now." It's not like Angela didn't know about it, but she hadn't seen Destiny since Walter Reed Hospital when gauze and bandages covered everything. She wrapped her right arm around her sister in a bear hug. A faint whiff of raspberries tickled her nose.

"Dezi, it's been so long. It's so good to see you settling in." Angela's voice didn't match the joy her words implied.

Destiny pulled away, staring at her. "I've been in Columbia over six months."

"Yeah." Angela waved her hand toward the little bungalow. "But you only recently moved in here, right? I had to see it. Congrats on your new home. I'm sorry I didn't bring you anything."

Seriously? Once they became adults, thanks to technology, they were great with Facetime, texting, and email, but since the hospital a year and a half ago, a new tension had developed between them. Yes, their lives had gone in completely different directions. With Destiny being the military brat and Angela the stereotypical princess, how much more different could they be? Was Destiny's injury making Angela uncomfortable? Destiny appreciated that Angela had come and sat by Destiny's bedside at Walter Reed for a week when she had first arrived stateside and then stuck by her through several surgeries. She valued it more than she could ever express. Saying their relationship was complicated was an understatement. Still, Destiny missed the camaraderie they once shared, even if by long distance. They'd made a vow to stay close, no matter what.

Before Walter Reed, they'd seen each other in person at Angela's wedding four years earlier. Destiny was overjoyed to be Angela's maid of honor. But she hadn't looking forward to spending time with Marlene, their mother.

Their relationship was more than complicated. As children, their parents' divorce and split in custody forced the children apart. In the beginning, the long-distance phone calls were juvenile. As they grew, communication waxed and waned in frequency, depending on what teen emergency was going on in Angela's life. Five years the senior, Destiny was supposed to have all the answers. After Angela's wedding, things improved, and there were more frequent emails, Facetime, and phone calls. Until

Afghanistan. To be fair, Destiny had been 7,000 miles away, and communication between the US and Afghanistan was shaky at best.

Destiny gave Angela her best smile despite the apprehension. "Okay, thanks, but a call or text with a heads-up would have been nice. What's going on?"

Tears rimmed Angela's eyes. Her lips turned down in a pout, and her blond hair flopped in front of her face. As she swiped at her hair with the back of her arm, light bounced off the three-carat solitaire on her left hand. Looking back at the cab pulling away, she said, "Well, if you don't want me here …"

Destiny grabbed her bags and slung them over her right shoulder. Thank God, she could still do that. Damn! What did she have in there? Rocks? "Don't be silly. Of course, I want you here. Come on in." She tried to remain calm, but the knot in her stomach said something was off. Angela looked wrong. They weren't the drop-in-any-time-without-notice kind of family.

Angela opened the door for her. "Oh, Dezi, this is darling. So quaint."

Was *quaint* a compliment or an insult? Most definitely the house wasn't like Angela's designer home in San Diego.

"You're so talented." Angela admired the paintings on the wall. "I could never do anything like this. I need a decorator to change the color in the bathroom."

Destiny almost smiled. There Angela was … the spoiled little rich girl. Could she simply want to visit? Destiny chastised herself. *I need to make a better effort at connecting with her. Communication is a two-way street.* Angela was all Destiny had now. She looked down at her left hand, then switched her gaze to her right. Having her military watch on her right wrist still felt awkward. Already late for her appointment at the clinic, she excused herself to make a quick phone call from the bedroom. "Sir, I'm so sorry. I'm not going to make it in today." Destiny peeked out through the crack in the doorway at her sister. "Something unexpected turned up. Please offer my apologies to the soldier waiting for me." She hated doing that, but what choice did she have?

Angela followed her into the kitchen. She sat across from Destiny at the shabby-chic mid-century Formica-top table for two. "Got any wine?"

Destiny glanced at her watch again. Eleven fifteen hours. Whoops—a quarter past eleven civilian time. "Isn't it a little early?"

Angela shrugged. A petite shoulder slipped from her snow-white cashmere sweater, exposing a lacy chartreuse bra strap. "Fine. Coffee then. You've always been so straightlaced. Try loosening up once in a while."

Destiny gritted her teeth. She didn't need a lecture, especially from Angela who'd never had a difficult day in her entire life. As sisters, they orbited in different galaxies. Angela had always been the flighty, devil-may-care sister, doted on by Marlene, while Destiny was the straight arrow, always taking life a little too seriously as the makeshift female in Dad's military household. Now, it felt all upended, even though Angela was one hundred percent dependent on her husband. Still, Angela was now the steady, stay-at-home-mom, and Destiny was … was what? Adrift? She dropped a filter into the coffee pot.

As the aroma of rich coffee beans filled the air, Angela filled Destiny in on life in San Diego. "Sam's as busy as ever, but with his long hours, I'm stuck with the kids 24-7."

The picture was forming. Angela's orthopedic surgeon husband, ten years her senior, was making tons of money, but Angela was left to raise their two-year-old twin girls and three-year-old son alone. Things not so perfect in forever land?

Angela nibbled on a chocolate chip cookie Destiny offered her from the cookie tin on the counter. "You can't begin to imagine how hard it is to find decent help. No one has a good work ethic anymore. Any little thing, and they don't show up."

Destiny retrained her irritation. "People have lives, Angela. Shit happens. Their kids get sick, cars break down. You have to be a little understanding." Angela was clueless to real problems in life. Things Destiny had seen in Afghanistan flashed through her mind. Sunni mothers scraping for food; or worse, patching body parts of their children after an explosion demolished their hut. After seeing all that, she had a hard time conjuring much sympathy for Angela.

"The last one walked out in the middle of the day," Angela continued. "No notice. No nothing." She huffed like it was the murder of the century.

Destiny fidgeted with the sleeve of her shirt, tugging it lower over the mechanical hand. She could swear sometimes it itched, which was clearly impossible. Why didn't Angela get to the point of why she was there? Was she going to ask if she and the kids could move in while she went through an extremely messy and expensive divorce? Destiny glanced around her tiny kitchen, and then got up to wipe the already spotless counter. Where would she put them?

She noticed Angela watching her move about the kitchen, her eyes glued to Destiny's prosthetic hand.

"Um … how do you make it work like that?" Angela asked.

The flesh-colored rubber covering of the mechanical hand wasn't pretty. "To be precise," said Destiny, "*it* is a myoelectric prosthesis. The muscles in my upper arm work with the electrodes fitted into the device. When I contract the muscles in my upper arm, it sends messages to my forearm and hand."

Angela nodded, but the expression on her face said she hadn't understood a word. "Was it hard to learn how to use it?"

Destiny flexed the fingers. The rubber hand hardly passed for the real thing. It was bulky and resembled a man's hand more than a woman's. Why couldn't they fit her with one that looked more feminine? "Yes, it's as much mental as medical. My brain had to learn to send the messages, and it certainly didn't happen overnight. The hand still doesn't always understand my signals or do what I want. But it's better than a hook or a fixed prosthetic." With her right hand, she placed a bright yellow happy-face mug in front of Angela. Destiny knew Angela wasn't there to talk about Destiny's arm. There had to be more to it than that.

"Ange, are you running away from Sam? Is that why you're here?"

Angela's head jerked up. "Oh, God, no. Sam's great. The kids are great. Well, mostly. Chelsea got sick while we were at Mom's, and I had to call Sam to come get them."

"Is she okay?" She meant Chelsea, not their mother. "Back up. You went to see Marlene? In Florida?" Destiny knew she was firing too many questions at once, but they spilled from her mouth.

"Chelsea is fine. Might have been a touch of the flu. And, yes, I went to see Mom. She's not good, Dezi. She needs your help."

The words *Mom* and *your help* together in one sentence slammed against Destiny's chest like a rocket mortar. *Mom?* Marlene was not her problem. They hadn't spoken more than a half-dozen words to each other in two decades. After years of arguing over it, Angela eventually acquiesced to never bringing up their mother. It was an unwritten rule. So why was Angela doing it now? Destiny fought back a surge of anger. "Ange, you know how I feel about Marlene."

Fresh tears smeared streaks of dark mascara down her sister's face. "She's your mother, too, you know. She needs help, and I couldn't stay there with three toddlers." Angela's breath came faster, and with each sentence, her voice raised another octave until the last words came out in a squeak. "Dezi. There's no one else. She needs … no, *I* need your help."

Destiny spun around. "Whoa. Why would Marlene need *me*?" The envelopes with the Florida return address flashed through Destiny's mind. Postmarked Florida, they came less frequently, but still arrived wherever she was. They had followed her to every base she lived on with Dad, to West Point, and into Afghanistan. Destiny never opened them, simply scribbled *Return to Sender* and mailed them back.

"What do you mean, she needs help? With what? Ange, you're not making any sense."

Angela wiped her face with a paper napkin from the handwoven basket on the table. "You need to see for yourself."

Destiny frowned. Whatever it was, Angela was clearly distraught. "See what?" Frustration mounted. Arms crossed across her chest, she leaned against the metal edge of the Formica countertop. "I need more information. Is she sick? Destitute? A drunk?"

Angela stared up at her, her mouth forming a perfect O. "Of course, she's not a drunk. How can you even say that?"

"Because I don't know her." Destiny shook her head. "So, what then? This doesn't make any sense. I need more."

They held eye contact for a moment that felt like a Mexican standoff. What was this unnamed thing? Sometimes Angela had been a bit of a flake, but she'd never been deceitful. "Is she mixed up in something illegal? Needs to be bailed out? Moving out of the country or something? Not coming back?" Destiny sat and ran her finger across the rim of her coffee cup. "I say good riddance. Florida isn't far enough as far as I'm concerned."

Angela slumped lower in the chair, looking even smaller than her five-foot-two self. "No, she's not moving. But she needs you. I need you to do this for *me*, if not for you."

For Angela? For herself? The whole idea was ridiculous. Destiny stood, grabbed the still-full coffee cups, and poured the contents into the sink. She replaced them with two stemmed wine glasses and filled both halfway with Chardonnay. Setting a glass in front of Angela, Destiny retreated against the counter and gulped down half the glass. "Why would she need me now?"

Angela raised an eyebrow and took a sip. "You'll see."

"Wait a minute," said Destiny. "Are you asking me to stay with her? As in *take care of her*? For how long? Why? She's only what, like sixty? Why would a sixty-year-old woman need help? You've got to be kidding." How dare Angela even ask? Destiny didn't *do* Marlene. The last time Destiny saw her mother was at Angela's wedding four years ago. Before that, at Dad's funeral in 2005. "You know better than that. If she needs a caretaker, I am most definitely not the candidate. Unless you're looking to hasten her death."

A look of horror crossed Angela's face.

"I'm kidding. I'm kidding. I wouldn't really kill her." Would she? No, of course not. No difference.

Marlene was already dead to her. "Ange, you know I'd do anything for you, but for her?" Destiny shook her head.

Angela got up from the table and stood only inches from Destiny.

Destiny tried to back up, but the counter hit her rear end. Talk about crossing into someone's personal space.

Angela held Destiny's good hand in hers. "Dezi, I'm asking this for *me,* not for her. There isn't anybody else. Won't you do this for me? I must get back to my own family, but we can't abandon her."

Abandon? Like she did to me? Not a good word choice to convince her. Destiny did love her sister, even if they had a strange, long-distance relationship. The day their mother had brought Angela home from the hospital was one of the happiest days in Destiny's life. Angela had been a sweet baby and a darling toddler. She'd let Destiny dress her up in silly costumes and feed her water and animal crackers in little plastic cups and plates. It had been like having a real-life doll. Until Marlene spirited her away.

Looking deeply into Angela's baby-blue eyes, under those fake designer eyelashes, Destiny saw someone on the brink of losing it. Her sister was a thirty-year-old mess. That was easy to see.

Destiny let out a deep breath. "Can't you hire someone for whatever this is? There must be someone else? Hasn't she remarried by now? She's not that old, and she's not my responsibility." The words tasted like grit as they came out of her mouth. Not that she didn't believe them, but even she heard how cold and heartless that sounded. "You've got to give me more to go on here."

Angela's face crumbled. She hiccupped. "P-l-e-a-s-e? There is no one else, at least no one we can count on. Go see her."

What did that mean? Destiny's mind raced. She had to find a way to get out of this. She'd gotten into a rhythm here in Columbia and begun to feel like a person, not a soldier. She no longer reached for Army green without thinking about it. She had a real hairdo and treated herself to mani/pedis on a regular basis. Acclimating had not been easy. She skirted the edges of PTSD, some days being significantly better than others. She never knew what would trigger a flashback and send her right back to the Middle East. It was time for her to think of herself, not her duty to others — especially not to Marlene. Destiny gulped down the rest of her wine. "If she's wanting to mend an old relationship with me, it's too late. It's been too late for an awfully long time now. I'd do anything else for you, you know that. But Marlene, no."

A flash of anger crossed Angela's face. "Well, I'm not asking for *anything else*." Her fingers did air quotes. "I'm asking for *this*." She slammed a hand on the counter.

Destiny jumped, the sound sending a flash of mortar fire through her body.

Angela paced in front of her. "Didn't I come and sit by your bedside at Walter Reed? Didn't I get Sam to refer you to the best orthopedic surgeon in the country?" She stopped inches from Destiny's nose. "I'm asking you to do this one thing for me. Please?"

It was true. Angela had been a good sister, and Destiny owed her. Angela had left her infant and toddler kids in California and sat by Destiny's bedside for a week. Considered one of the best orthopedic surgeons in the nation, Sam's opinion was respected. Not that it had saved her arm. Nobody could perform miracles. Still, she owed them a debt of gratitude.

Angela dropped her head into her hands. "Look. I know I'm not the best wife or mother or sister. But right now, I feel like the world's worst daughter." She dabbed at her eyes with a napkin. "I made Sam fly clear across the country and get the kids at Mom's in Florida, and I came straight here to South Carolina. I don't know what I'll do if you don't say yes."

Oh, no, she was not going to play the good-daughter/bad-daughter game. Guess who would lose that one? Destiny paced the room. She had to think. What was going on that Angela refused to tell her? Was Marlene dying? Did Destiny care? She tossed that idea around in her head for a second. No, she didn't wish that on her mother. Not even Destiny was that cold.

"It's your last chance, you know," Angela said through her tears. "If it's not already too late."

Destiny stopped pacing. "Last chance for what?"

"You know, to find out why."

Destiny waved the idea away with the swish of her hand. Whatever. It didn't matter. Destiny didn't care anymore. Marlene had left, taking Angela and abandoning Destiny. What else was there to say?

Angela twisted the napkin in her hand. "You know, she said she had no choice. And she always loved you."

Destiny snorted. "Yeah, right. Mother-of-the-Year she was not."

That flash of anger again. "And what about fathers?" snapped Angela. "After the divorce, I never received so much as a birthday card from Dad. It was like I never existed."

Destiny's spine stiffened, and her phantom arm began to itch. "Hey, Dad was the only person in the world I could count on. Don't even think about making him the bad guy in this."

"Well, he wasn't so great for me."

Destiny hadn't ever thought of it that way. How selfish. Perhaps she was being too hard on Angela. Destiny had her own issues. She was an adult now. Why couldn't she let it go? Guilt crept up the back of her neck like a spider. Did she owe Angela this one request? Destiny was a soldier. She'd faced enemy fire and survived. She could endure their mother for one week. How hard could it be?

Reluctantly, she nodded.

Two

The plane taxied down the runway at zero nine hundred and climbed into the sky. Sucking in a deep breath, Destiny watched Columbia disappear under the clouds as the plane veered south. As she had before going into battle, she steeled herself for the worst, hoped for the best.

Whatever awaited her, this was going to be a quick trip. If her mother wanted to make amends, it was too late. If it was financial, there was little Destiny could do to help. Angela and Sam were the ones with all the money. There had to be more to the situation than that. Angela had been so mysterious.

The woman across the aisle gave Destiny one of those sympathetic looks she hated, so she tucked her prosthetic hand under her scarf. After a moment's thought, she stared the woman straight in the eye and pulled the scarf back off, exposing her hand and wrapped the scarf around her neck. *Yes, I'm an amputee, a freak. Need a better look?*

The woman blanched and turned away.

Good.

The plane gained altitude above the clouds, blinding her with the sudden brilliant sunlight.

Destiny pulled down the shade on the window beside her. What if Marlene was in a homeless shelter, strung out on drugs or alcohol? Wouldn't Angela have said that? There had to be something else. Okay then, what about her health? Is that what Angela meant about *last time*? Destiny did the math. Marlene was only fifty-five years old. Unless she had some grave terminal illness. That was unlikely. Whatever it was, the sooner Destiny confronted the issue and got out of town the better.

After this, the score would be settled between her and Angela. Destiny would not fall for that trap again. Priority number one—reconnaissance. She should have pushed Angela with more questions. Destiny wasn't a very proficient interrogator. Not like Max. Were her military instincts slipping? Who goes into battle half-assed? She was blindly taking orders, behaving more like a private, or worse, a civilian, than a commissioned officer. What was the first thing she needed to do when she got there? A strange mission. This felt a lot like deployment—everything on a need-to-know basis. She could only hope for a quick in-and-out mission.

Destiny closed her eyes and tried to picture her mother. The last time she had seen her was at Angela's wedding, four years ago. Marlene's floor-length icy blue gown. *Just like her heart.* The same blond hair Destiny remembered from years ago. She didn't look fifty. She could have easily passed as Destiny's older sister.

There was so much Destiny didn't know. Was her mother living alone? Did she know Destiny was coming? Only Angela would cook up something like this to get them to reconcile. Destiny slammed her prosthetic hard on the armrest. That was it! *Damn you, Angela. Great act. You should go into acting.*

The lady across the aisle startled, then glared at her.

Oh, go to hell. Destiny gave the woman a death stare, then returned to her own thoughts.

Angela, the peacemaker, couldn't stand having her family torn apart. It'd been impossible to fix things when Destiny was overseas, but now that she was home, Angela had made her move, and Destiny had fallen right into the trap. This was all about Angela's planned mother-daughter reconciliation. *Not going to work, little sister.*

One-handed, Destiny fumbled, pulling the rucksack from beneath the chair in front of her then struggled to find a pen and paper to scribble a list.

Find a hotel room, close to Marlene's. No way was Destiny going to stay with her mother.

Find out what the hell this was about.

Get the hell out of Dodge.

What else?

Lists, like labels, reminded her of the mother of her childhood. The Label Queen. The Dymo-label maker was Marlene's favorite household appliance. Destiny also enjoyed the order found in making lists and labeling things. Her file cabinet at home was testament to that. She checked the small list again. The comfort she usually found in them wasn't there. The little info she had wasn't worth writing down. She crumpled the paper and tossed it in the trash bag the flight attendant offered for cups and peanut bags.

The hour-and-a-half flight landed in Fort Myers all too soon. Humidity smacked her in the face the second she stepped off the small two-prop plane. *Why on earth would anyone want to live in this?* The sooner she got back to South Carolina, the better. According to the car rental attendant, it was an hour's drive to Marco Island. Destiny threw her rucksack into the back seat and cranked up the A/C.

The radio offered two choices: country or Latin. No pop? Country, it was. A Garth Brooks song filled the car with sound and memories. Her throat tightened. Their mother used to sing that song. She'd tell Destiny and Angela the song was about them, not about a man. Would they always know she loved them if tomorrow never came? Destiny would laugh and say she was being silly. *What a crock of shit.* Marlene *did* stop loving her—and tomorrow *had* come, without Marlene. Exasperated, Destiny clicked off the radio and enjoyed the quiet. The sun glistened off the Gulf of Mexico as she crested the Judge Jolley Bridge onto the island. The view was pretty: sailboats with tall white masts, a parasailer with a rainbow sail, and gleaming yachts in a pristine harbor. She smiled to herself at the Key-West style homes with pastel siding and circular driveways lined in palm trees. Nice. Rolling down the window, she inhaled the salt air and breeze from the Gulf.

The only hotels on the island were high-priced tourist traps on the beach, but the view from her room at the Hilton was to die for. She stepped onto the small balcony, and a cool breeze wrapped around her, so different from the oppressive heat at the airport. Waves of sparkling blue water splashed in a crescent-shaped, white-sanded beach. Inviting tiki huts with thatched roofs to relax in the shade called to her. Perhaps she'd steal a little time to dip her toes in the water before she left. She pulled herself back to reality. She wasn't there to vacation. She was on a mission.

She checked her military watch. Fifteen Thirty. *No, not 1530, 3:30 p.m.* She could find plenty of reasons to put off this reunion if she tried. She could check her email messages, browse Facebook, take that walk on the beach, dip her toes in the Gulf. No. No time like the present to face her enemy. Shutting the door to her room, she braced herself for the unknown.

The GPS in the white Taurus directed her to Marlene's condo on the northwest side of the island in an area they called Olde Marco, even though she didn't see a single thing exceptionally old about it. Her mother's ground floor unit was tucked in a two-story U-shaped building behind bright red bougainvillea bushes and backed up to a canal that led out to the Gulf of Mexico. Unit 103-A. *Like on those damn envelopes.* And here it was, staring into her face. Destiny brushed a stray hair from her face where the humidity glued it in place and rapped on the door.

No answer. She expelled a breath with relief. She turned to leave as the door swung open.

A brown-skinned man with gleaming white teeth and a body right out of *GQ* magazine smiled at her. Dressed in pale green hospital scrubs, he stretched a slender hand in her direction. "Oh, you must be Miss Destiny. Miss Angela said you'd be coming today."

"Uh …" Destiny sputtered. Angela had never mentioned anything about a man. She tugged at her not-short, not-yet-long strands of straight brown hair. "I'm Captain … err … Destiny Osgood. I'm sorry. I wasn't expecting …" *What was she expecting?* Certainly not this.

"Ah, you were expecting an old, gray-haired white nursemaid?" His dark eyes twinkled. "Good timing. I just got here myself. Come in. I'm Enrique. Your mama is expecting you. She's having a good day today."

Nursemaid? Her mama? What was going on? Never in her thirty-five years had Destiny ever referred to her mother as *Mama*. Mommy, Mom, Mother, Bitch, Marlene, but never Mama. Mama was reserved for those you had a special affinity for. Someone you loved. Someone who loved you. "Wait," said Destiny. "Let's call her Marlene, shall we? And you're going to have to start from the beginning. Who are you, and why does she need a nurse?"

Enrique's face clouded, and he bit his lip. He held the door wider for her to enter. "I'm not a nurse. I'm Miss Marlene's home health aide. Come in."

Inside the small living room/dining room combination, everything was pristine—at first glance. The small, tufted-linen sofa and matching chairs looked copied right out of *Southern Living* magazine. Bamboo and cane accents gave everything a tropical flair. But things seemed a bit off. Items were in odd places: an umbrella hanging from a light fixture in the small dining room, a straw hat over a lamp shade, a pair of slippers on top of the stove. Very peculiar.

Enrique scurried around picking up the odd items and putting them in their rightful place, mumbling his apologies for not having had time to pick up before she arrived.

But what caught Destiny's attention, the true beauty in the condo, were the charcoal sketches of the sea and canvases pulled tight on raised frames. Destiny could recognize her mother's drawings anywhere. No sign of the artist, or her *Mama*, as Enrique had called her.

Enrique pointed down a narrow hallway. "Come this way, pór favor. She's in the bedroom."

Destiny held out her hand in a motion to stop. "Wait. I don't understand."

Now Enrique looked confused. "What don't you understand, Miss Destiny?"

"Anything."

Without answering, he gestured to what Destiny assumed was a bedroom. "Come, she's waiting."

Suddenly self-conscious of how she looked, Destiny ran a sweaty palm across her white denim skirt and tugged at the left sleeve of her button-down blouse. Did she still look like woman with a bionic man-hand? Why was she nervous? Marlene meant nothing to her. Destiny stepped into a room of soothing sea-foam green. A wall of glass across from her gave the room a spacious feel, allowing a great view of a green, neatly trimmed lawn, sparkling pool, and a half-dozen or so boats on lifts in a canal.

Marlene sat in a floral slipper chair by the sliding glass door, staring out at who-knows-what. She didn't turn when Destiny came in. Marlene's hair was still blond, with a little help from a bottle now, cut short, but stylish. Even without seeing her face straight-on, she still seemed younger than her age, dressed fashionably, albeit not to Destiny's taste.

Mr. Hunk-of-a-man gave Marlene's small shoulders a squeeze.

For some reason, Destiny didn't like it. Why was he touching her like that?

"Miss Marlene," he said softly.

Destiny conceded he had a beautiful accent.

"She's here, your daughter, Destiny. Isn't it wonderful? She's here." He turned to Destiny. His high wattage smile could turn on a light bulb.

Marlene didn't turn or acknowledge Destiny's presence.

Destiny waited. What should she do? Stand there all day? Why wouldn't Marlene look at her?

His dazzling smile vanished. He held up a finger and walked around to kneel in front of Marlene. "Miss Marlene. You were telling me about your daughter, Destiny, earlier today." He grabbed the sides of her chair and turned her to face Destiny.

Destiny stood motionless as Marlene's eyes wandered over her body, starting at her sandaled feet. Her mother's gaze moved up her legs, over her thighs, across her stomach, over her breasts. Agonizingly slowly. Like a platoon inspection, Destiny forced herself to stay rooted in place, arms straight at her side. Marlene's gaze traveled to Destiny's left arm and mechanical hand. She assumed an at-ease pose with both hands clasped behind her back. Marlene settled on Destiny's face, paused there, then finally, their gazes met. The muscles in Destiny's legs twitched. Her impulse was to run. She felt trapped in a fox hole.

For God's sake, Marlene. Say something. Why was Destiny's body betraying her this way? Her left 'hand' twitched uncontrollably on its own. She clasped it tighter with her good hand. She wasn't scared to see her mother. She was only here as a favor to Angela.

Marlene's brows knitted together. She tilted her head to one side and pursed her lips. Her blue eyes showed no signs of recognition. She inspected Destiny again, her gaze traveling down her body and then back up to her face.

It had been four years, but wouldn't a mother still recognize her own daughter? What was going on here? Why? What had she been expecting? What did this mean, and why did she care? They meant nothing to each other. Did she expect some kind of tearful reunion? Destiny's insides wilted though her body stayed rigid, ramrod straight at attention, even in an at-ease position.

Marlene turned her head toward Enrique. Life filtered into her eyes, and she crooked an index finger for him to come closer. She pointed a slender finger with hot pink nails in Destiny's direction. "Who's that?"

Three

Destiny still didn't know why Angela had been so secretive about Marlene's condition and Enrique hadn't alleviated Destiny's apprehensions. Still, the way he touched Marlene, how his voice went soft when he addressed her made Destiny uncomfortable. Did this gorgeous man genuinely care for her? What was in it for him? Or was he a gold digger hoping to get an inheritance? He was quite a bit younger than Marlene, but he wouldn't be the first young stud hoping to live off the luxuries of an older woman's hard work. Destiny would have to keep her eye on him. She didn't know her mother's financial situation, but she was pretty sure he'd be in for a big disappointment.

Marlene had certainly never showered Destiny with any extravagances growing up. Had she been different with Angela? *After.* A twinge of something tugged at her gut. Was that churning jealousy? Of Enrique? Of Angela? Ridiculous.

Enrique tried again. "Miss Marlene, that's Destiny, your daughter." He glanced at Destiny, narrowing his eyes as though to apologize. "It happens like this sometimes. Try talking to her." He offered Destiny a straight-backed chair beside her mother.

What happens like this sometime? Destiny walked over, less steady on her legs than when she fought in Afghanistan and sat down. "Hello. It's been a long time. Chelsea was sick, and Angela needed to get back to San Diego, so she asked me to check in on you."

Marlene's eyes searched Destiny's. Her mother opened and closed her mouth like a fish gasping for air. If she understood what Destiny was saying, she didn't acknowledge it. Then she turned her face away from Destiny, back toward the sliding glass door, dismissing her once again.

The seconds ticked away in silence. Destiny tamped down the urge to scream at her. *Say something.* Her phantom hand twitched again. Should she say more? Leave the room? Walk away?

Enrique cocked his head in the direction of the door, and Destiny followed him into the tiny galley kitchen, grateful to be away from the awkward situation.

"I'm so sorry she doesn't recognize you." He leaned in whispering. He was close, too close. She could smell his manly citrus cologne. She retreated a step until her back touched the countertop.

"I was sure she would," he continued. If he was aware of Destiny's backstep, he didn't acknowledge it. "She was talking about you moments before you arrived. She said you liked to draw, and you did it together all the time. So, you're an artist too." It wasn't a question.

An emptiness filled Destiny's stomach. "That was a very, very long time ago. And I don't mean to be rude, but I still don't understand. Why doesn't she recognize me?" She pressed her lips together and inhaled through her nose. "And again, why does she need a home health aide?"

"Oh, Miss Destiny. I'm sorry. I thought Miss Angela would have explained. Miss Marlene has Alzheimer's Disease." He dipped his head as if in an apology.

Destiny balked and shook her head. "Alzheimer's? No, you must be mistaken. She's only fifty-five years old."

"It's true. It's called early onset Alzheimer's. Only about 5% of Alzheimer patients, those under sixty years of age, fall in this category. I'm here to help her with basic needs, like remembering how to dress and use things like her toothbrush or table utensils. It's my job to help her keep those skills as long as possible. Like an occupational therapist, but without the degree."

Wait. What? "She can't dress herself?" The words came out in a squeak. Destiny tried to remember what little she knew of Alzheimer's. She recalled that the people affected had memory lapses. But this? She'd had no idea. Angela hadn't been fair. She should have given Destiny a warning.

"Sometimes she can, and at other times, she needs some help."

Destiny glanced through the doorway at the woman sitting and staring out the slider. She was dressed stylishly and was well groomed. At least that was good. Enrique must have been taking good care of her. She wouldn't have to concern herself too much if things were already taken care of.

"Do you live here with her?"

"Oh, no," he said. "I only come three days a week for one-hour sessions. That is all Medicaid covers. Miss Angela was here last week. Sometimes, Philip comes by. And she has a fine neighbor who checks in on her. But to be honest, Miss Marlene is going downhill quicker than we'd hoped. She shouldn't be living alone. In the last month, she's recognizing fewer and fewer people and places. I'm so glad you are here to look after her now."

Destiny cringed. Florence Nightingale, she was not.

"Ernesto—"

"Enrique."

"Yes, sorry. Enrique. I do appreciate what you are doing for Marlene. But I'm not here to stay on any permanent basis. And who is Philip?"

A frown creased his brow. "Philip's her boy-friend." He spat it like it was a dirty word. Enrique leaned in close. "I don't trust him."

"I see." Destiny had no idea Marlene had a boy-friend. But of course, there was little Destiny knew about her mother anymore. "And why don't you trust him?"

Enrique fiddled with the clasp on his backpack. "It's not my place to say, but—"

"But what, Enrique?" She was getting impatient with him. *Could it be he was homing in on the fortune you hoped to score?*

"Well, he's conveniently not available when she needs real help. He runs for the hills on the days she's not lucid. But give her a good day, and he's all over her like salsa on chips. Doesn't act sincere to me."

Destiny nodded. "I see," she said again. "Well, if she can't be left alone, the next best thing is to get her into a home. And please, call me Destiny, or Captain if you insist. Drop the Miss."

His dark eyes went a shade darker. Was that anger? "Miss Destiny—"

She raised her hand to stop him from whatever was going to come out of his mouth. She knew she wouldn't want to hear it.

He continued as if he didn't see her hand signal. "Miss Destiny, Miss Marlene is a wonderful woman. Most of those places are dark, depressing pits filled with ghost people waiting to die. Your mama is young. You don't want her in those places, believe me. She will remember you. Give her time. I promise."

Destiny didn't know who he thought this wonderful woman was, but that wouldn't be her description of Marlene. He was only Marlene's aide and had met her when her memory was already shattered. Stories about drawing pictures with her daughter would have sounded loving to a stranger.

Of course, this did little to help Destiny figure out what to do with her. Marlene didn't appear to be able to function alone in this place, no matter how helpful her neighbors were. And, if Enrique was right, this Philip guy didn't sound like a winner either. Whether Enrique liked it or not, institutionalization seemed the best option. That would be tomor-row's mission. Find a place to put Marlene.

Four

Marlene

I'm holding a driver's license in my hand with a picture of a woman. She looks like an older version of me, or what I imagine I will look like. Ugh. Not good. That can't be me. But it has my name on it. The birthdate says June 21,1966. That's right. It must be me. I walk over to the mirror. That same older woman is looking back at me. Leaning in closer, I trace my fingers down the wrinkles around the eyes, other frown lines that crease the jowls. My heart does a little leap into my throat. I can't breathe. When did I get old? Suddenly I'm woozy and grip the dresser to steady myself. I might faint. I don't want to see that vision in the mirror anymore and sit back down on the edge of the bed. What's happening to me?

Looking back down at the license, I wonder *how old does that make me?* What year is it anyway? And why do I have this in my hand? Was I going somewhere? Oh, yes, I've got an appointment this week with the director of Trump Towers in Miami to do some paintings for the building. What day is that? I'll check my planner. This could be the project that sets me up for the rest of my life. As I tuck it back into the wallet in my lap and shove it into the handbag at my feet; I notice an ID bracelet on my wrist. *Memory Impaired. Call 9-1-1.*

Memory Impaired. My heart skips a beat. My God, could this be real? Am I losing my mind? It couldn't be.

A noise comes from the kitchen. "Who's there?" I call out. I'm not expecting anyone. "Philip? Is that you?" He's been so distant lately. Perhaps it's Claire Johnson from next door. She's a sweet old lady, always bringing me home-made goodies. I do enjoy our time together, sipping tea and nibbling on her home-made cookies. "Claire, is that you?"

A dark head peeks around the corner. "No, it's me, Destiny. I'm heating up some of this great looking chicken cacciatore Mrs. Johnson left for you. What would you like to drink with your meal?"

Did she say Destiny? My Destiny? That grown woman couldn't be her. Destiny is a teenager. Why is she here? "Um." I can't decide. My chest tightens, threatening to squeeze the life right out of me. What's happening to me? I finger my earrings and smooth a hand over my hair. Did I lose five years, ten? My chest tightens. I can't breathe. I straighten my shirt. I'm a successful artist, a strong independent woman. That must be what she sees. Slowly, I make my way out of the bedroom.

The woman emerges from the kitchen into the dining area with two plates balanced on my favorite pink flamingo potholder mitts. She sets them down on the table and pulls out a chair. I know I'm staring. There's something familiar about her, but the pieces don't come together to make any sense. Short brown hair pokes out around her ears. She's tall and muscular on a trim frame. Could it really be Destiny? She operates with confidence, as if she's in the right place, so maybe it is. But how? Damn it. This can't be happening.

"Here, Mar, is this where you sit?" She contemplates the two chairs. "Or is this your seat?" She sets the plates down and slips off the mitts.

"Ahh—" I stifle a scream. She has an artificial hand, some mechanical thing with an unrealistic rubber covering that's supposed to look like skin. It's huge, like a man's hand, like something out of a horror movie. I look away and take the first seat offered and pull my sweater over my ID bracelet. It's the wrong seat, but I let that slide.

"It's okay to look." The woman holds out the atrocious hand. It flexes, the fingers moving jerkily. How does she do that? Her eyes meet mine for a split second. There is a definite familiarity in them, but a reserved distance too.

"It's mechanical," she says, "and moves from sensory signals I send from my brain. It can do almost everything my real hand could do."

How did she end up with a fake hand? A car accident? I'll go along and see if I can catch a clue, see if it is her or an imposter. "Destiny. This is quite a surprise. I didn't know you were coming." I reach across the table to take her hand, her real one. She pulls away and tucks it under the table, but not before I noticed the callouses. The short square nails. Not the hand of a dainty woman. This girl knows hard work.

Her eyebrows knit together. "We had a long conversation before dinner. You, me, and Enrique. Remember?" She jumps up. "Oh, I nearly forgot. You like red wine with dinner."

I don't. And who is Enrique? I want to know, but I won't ask. My head is spinning. That bracelet on my wrist is exposed, so I tug my sleeve down. "Oh, yes. You and your friend, Enrique. Such a nice man."

"Uh, Enrique and I aren't" — she shrugs — "It doesn't matter." She pours the wine and concentrates on her chicken.

Okay. If that man — what did she say his name was, oh yes, Enrique — isn't Destiny's boyfriend, *if this really is Destiny*, then who is he? Should I ask? Would that be prying? If she *is* my daughter, I should be able to ask. "Destiny, I didn't mean to meddle. It was a simple deduction. It's fine if you don't want to say you're in a relationship."

Her mouth drops open. Then she laughs, a big belly-laugh like Destiny did when she was a child. Maybe this *is* her, all grown up. "No," she says. "I met Enrique a few minutes ago. He's your home health aide." A gleam shows in her eyes. "But I'll admit, he *is* cute."

I force a smile. My what? Why do I need a home health aide? If we had this conversation a few hours ago, why can't I remember? I reach for my knife and fork and stop short. Oh no, what now? Do I hold the knife in my left hand and the fork in the right, or the other way around? I pick them up and stare at them, then switch them, then switch them back. My cheeks burn. This is ridiculous. A grown woman that can't cut her own meat. I look up to see if she's watching. If she sees, at least she's not openly gawking. She's concentrating on her plate. Her left hand — that mechanical thing — is tucked under the table in her lap, and she's breaking her chicken apart with the fork in her right hand. I follow her lead, set the knife down and press into the chicken with my fork. Thank goodness, it falls apart easily.

Destiny casts a sideways glance at me. She asks about the island and my friends. "I understand you have a special friend, Philip, I think. Tell me about him."

A special friend? She makes it sound like something childish, or worse, sordid. "Yes, Philip is my boyfriend. We've been together several years now. I'm surprised he's not here now. Did he call while I was napping? I'm sorry about that. What kind of hostess am I?" *Damn. I'm rambling. Pull it together, Marlene.*

"No, there's been no call from him, but I'm looking forward to meeting him. Tell me about him."

As sure as I knew, I suddenly don't. I know the name. I know he's my guy. But I don't remember anything about him and can't even place what he looks like. My heart's beating hard against my chest again. Am I having a heart attack? Or a stroke?

Destiny jumps from the chair and comes around the table as if she's going to pick me up off the floor. "Marlene, are you all right? You're flushed."

"No, no. I'm fine." I try to laugh, but it comes out fake. "Hot flashes." I wave a hand in front of my face.

Destiny looks closely at me, then retakes her seat across from me.

My heart rate returns to normal, and I suddenly remember: *Knife in right hand. You cut with your right hand.* I take a sip of the red wine. It's good. I guess I like red wine after all.

"Have you talked to Angela lately?" I ask. If she was who she claims to be, she'd know who that is. I'm hoping her answer will provide a clue about her visit.

"Yes, Angela's sorry she couldn't stay any longer, but she needed to get home. Little Chelsea must have caught a bug while she was here. I hope she didn't give it to you. I bet it was fun to see them all. Instead, you're stuck with me for a while."

I try to disguise my shock by hiding my mouth behind a napkin. *Angela has kids? They were here? Who is Chelsea?* For how long? A day, a week? And now Destiny. She hasn't spoken to me since … since when? Has she ever answered my letters? Why can't I remember? Have we reconciled? I scrutinize her face. No clues. Does she know the truth? Can we talk about it? No, no. What if I'm wrong? If she doesn't know, why is she here? We need to talk. I could ruin this by saying the wrong things.

She's sitting at my table sharing chicken cacciatore. She must know. She must have forgiven me, and I don't remember. Miracles never cease. God could throw in one more and return my memory.

The next morning, the sound of children squealing with glee wake me from a strange dream, something about Destiny — all grown — visiting me. Funny what dreams can do. They can make all your wishes come true. Silly me. I look out the window. A man I recognize, but can't name, is loading five children into a pontoon boat. Better him than me. They are a handful, loud and rambunctious.

I've got to get going if I'm going to drive over to Miami today. A commission for sixteen paintings. They want acrylics. Not my favorite medium, but for the money I'm contracted for, I'd use finger paints if they asked. What should I wear? My God. Donald Trump. What luck that one of his staff vacationed at the JW Marriott here on Marco Island and saw my art and he inquired about them. Such a stroke of luck. He, Mr. Trump, not the staff member, is running for President of the United States. If he's elected, will I be doing paintings for the White House next?

There is a photo on my nightstand I don't remember. Where did that come from? There's a picture of three children, twin little girls and a boy. Who are they? I should know who they are, but the more I stare at the photo, the less I understand. Since their picture is here, they must be important to me. Focus. My children? Grandchildren? I don't know them. I blink away tears, look down at the bracelet on my wrist. This can't be happening. I hate this! I hate this! I hate this! I toss the photo across the room. The frame smashes against the wall, the glass shattering into a thousand pieces.

Five

Destiny awoke to a loud crash. Enemy fire? She reached for her weapon with her left arm and found air, no weapon, no hand. A righty for everything else, she'd always been a lefty with a weapon. She glanced around. Breathed a sigh of relief. She wasn't in the field; she was in her mother's condo in Florida.

She rushed from her spot on the pull-out sofa to her mother's room and found a shattered picture frame, the glass broken in tiny shards on the tile floor. "Marlene, what happened?"

From the look on her mother's face, she had no idea who Destiny was. Where was Enrique or Angela, or even Philip, when she needed them?

Destiny sucked in a breath. A picture frame does not fly off a dresser by itself. "It's okay. Stay on the bed until I sweep this up. There's glass every-where. We don't want you to get cut." The loose flap of her left shirt sleeve slapped her side as she turned to find a broom and dustpan. Perhaps in the kitchen?

Marlene's eyes bulged. "Get out of my house," she screamed. "I'll call the police. I don't have any-thing to steal." She clutched her nightgown around her, terror in her eyes, like she was looking at the one-armed killer in *The Fugitive*. "Philip. Philip. Help!"

Whoa. Destiny slowed her movements and lowered her voice to be less threatening like she'd learned in military confrontations. She crossed her good arm over her stump. She recognized that look of fear. A vision of tattered Sunni children, their eyes wide with fear, flashed through her mind. She held up her right hand in the universal symbol of surrender. "I'm not going to hurt you. It's me, Destiny, your daughter. You're safe. I only want to clean up the broken glass." She pointed to the shards on the floor by the window. "See?"

Marlene followed her gaze, then clutched the covers tighter over her chest. "How did you get in here? You're not my Destiny. Where's Philip? Did you do something to him?" She abruptly threw the blanket off her legs and tried to stand. "Get out of my house." Her eyes blazed with fury.

Dear God. Why am I dealing with this? Marlene is not my job. Destiny looked for any action from Marlene. Was she looking for a weapon? She didn't seem to know where she was. Destiny needed to deescalate the situation and do it fast. Temporarily giving up on the cleanup, Destiny walked two steps away but blocked the doorway, giving Marlene a little extra space. *Go along with whatever place she is in.* "Philip stepped out for a few minutes. He'll be back soon. You're safe. I'm not going to hurt you."

Destiny watched as Marlene eased back onto the bed. She pulled the covers back over her too-pale-for-Florida legs. Marlene's eyes clouded, and she stared over Destiny's shoulder. Destiny wasn't sure Marlene was there anymore. She'd gone somewhere else in her mind.

The crisis abated for now, Destiny went in hunt of the broom, stopping first to attach her prosthesis. *Thank God, it was still charged.* She found the broom and dustpan to sweep up the glass. The broom was no problem, but twice the dustpan slipped from her artificial grip and dropped to the floor. *Damn!* Finally, she achieved her mission and tip-toed back into the kitchen. The morning's crisis had left her shaken. She needed to talk to Angela. She punched the speed dial on her iPhone and let it ring. It went to voicemail. "Ange, call me as soon as you get this." She hung up and repeated the same message in a text.

Seconds later, her screen lit up with a text.
What's up? Mom okay?

Far from it. What the hell, Ange? You know that. Please call me.

Can it wait? Trying to get kids to eat. Will call soon as I get them settled.

OK. Destiny replied.

She didn't mean it. She slipped her skirt on over her wrinkled blouse and flipped on the coffee pot. *God, what a morning.* She did the math. Zero 912 = 9:12 *a.m.* EST, late for her. It must have been the lack of sleep on the tiny pull-out bed. It was only 6:12 in San Diego. Angela's days started early. Destiny didn't envy her lifestyle, but at the moment, she didn't like her own so well either. She folded up the bed, filled a mug with coffee, and dropped unto the sofa, careful not to spill on the light fabric. Angela.

Destiny was going to ring her sister's neck. How dare she not mention this early onset Alzheimer's. Destiny gulped down the coffee.

Her phone rang with the "Hotel California" ringtone. Angela. Jumping off the sofa, Destiny slammed her knee into the coffee table while reaching for her phone on the kitchen counter. *Shit.*

Rubbing her knee, she grabbed her phone just in time. "Angela?"

"Hey. You scared me calling so early. Is Mom okay?"

"Hardly. She thought I was a burglar or something." Destiny relayed the details of the incident. "I don't know who was more freaked out, her or me. You were holding out on me, weren't you? Not cool, little sister."

Destiny felt more than heard the pause in Angela's answer. "Well, it was different every day. No point in giving you the worst picture before you got there. I knew you'd figure it out. Always the soldier, right?"

Destiny huffed, trying to tamp down her anger. She'd been duped. "This isn't the same thing at all, and you know it."

"Sorry."

Angela didn't sound a bit sorry, but it wouldn't solve anything to get into a quarrel over the phone about it. All she could do is take charge. "So, tell me about this Philip guy. What's his story?"

"Ah, Philip. What an asshole. I only met him twice. He acted like he didn't want me there, but I definitely didn't feel like it was because he wanted to take care of her himself. He's this wanna-be performer on the island. Never made it any farther than singing for his supper at the local hotels. Mom met him when she was doing the artwork for the JW."

Destiny snorted. "Great, can't wait to meet him. Listen, Ange, we need a plan. Is she financially solid? As in, able to pay for long term care? That will be a lot of dough. And we can't let Prince Philip get his hands on any of it. Could you and Sam pay for long-term care indefinitely? I know I can't. I've got to find her accounts and insurance papers. Do you know where any of that is?"

Angela exhaled deeply into the phone. "No idea. Did you look in the bookcase?

Destiny hurried over to it. A bookshelf held lots of books, author names she'd never heard of: Randy Wayne White, Karl Hiaasen, T. Milton Mayer, and Elizabeth Perdichizzi. A beautiful coffee-table book of Florida landscape photographs by Rich Blonna. Glancing at the backs, she noticed they were all local Floridian authors.

She found stacks of loose papers in a deep drawer below the bookcase. She sat cross-legged on the floor and pulled a stack into her lap, her phone still balanced between her shoulder and her ear. She rattled off her findings to her sister. "Oh, Ange, electric bill, past due, a letter from the condo association, late on condo fees, phone bill, also past due. Marlene hasn't paid anything for months. It's a wonder everything hasn't been cut off. They're all past due."

She pulled a Social Security statement from the pile showing a monthly allotment of $946.00 per month.

"Here's a Social Security statement. Did you help her set that up? She's too young for Social Security retirement benefits. This must be a disability statement. There must be another income, wouldn't you think? She can't be living on $946.00 a month."

Angela gasped over the phone. "A month? Are you sure it's not a week? Who can live on that? She had income from her art. I know she had a big contract with the J.W. Marriott. All the artwork in the hotel is hers. When they remodeled a few years ago, they commissioned her to draw beach and city scenes of the island. Then they made prints out of them and put them in all the guest suites. The originals are in the lobby, restaurants, and conference rooms. She really is ... or *was* talented."

With only two major hotels on the island, Destiny had picked the wrong one to stay in. Had she chosen the J.W. Marriott; she would have seen her mother's work. No doubt she would have recognized them immediately.

"Well, that gives me something to search for anyway. She's not good. How dare you do this to me? What were you thinking? I can't take care of her myself."

"It was the only thing I knew to do. I wasn't sure you'd go if I told you all of it at once."

She was right. Would Destiny have come given all the details? "Well, I've got to find someone or some place for her."

"I found a place," said Angela. "But there is a waiting list. Can you stay until—"

"No," Destiny shouted, a little too loudly. "What about her doctors? Who are they? Can I talk to them, get some help or advice from them?"

"Enrique can probably help you with that. Somebody must be paying him to see Mom." She giggled; a simple childish laugh Destiny remembered from a long time ago. "Speaking of Enrique—what do you think of him? Talk about a hottie. If I wasn't married …"

As angry as Destiny was with her, she couldn't help but smile. It diffused the moment a little. "You'd do what? Marry a Mexican home health aide and live on love? You own shoes that cost more than a month's wages for him."

"Argentinian," Angela corrected. "Well, I could have a passionate fling. Did you see those arms? And you could break rocks on those pecs. Honestly, Dezi, have you jumped his bones yet?"

The cold coffee Destiny was sipping spewed out of her mouth. "Angela! First, he's Marlene's aide, that's it. Second, I just got here. And third, he's rather pushy and not my type." *As if he'd ever be interested in a plain GI Jane like me with a stump for an arm anyhow. Now Angela, yeah.*

"He can push me anywhere, anytime, if you ask me."

Destiny cleared her throat. "We're talking about Marlene, not Enrique. He practically forced me to stay here last night after he ran out on me and left me alone with her. I slept on this stupid little pull-out bed when I had a wonderful queen size bed at the Hilton. I don't even have a toothbrush here. I need to shower and get clean clothes, and I'm afraid to leave her alone for more than a few minutes. I had to fix her dinner and remind her to brush her teeth before bed. At least she was able to undress and get her own nightgown on."

"He can't stay overnight, you know. I know it's not easy," said Angela, "and I do appreciate you doing this. Try looking through her nightstand. I think I remember seeing some sort of metal box in her bedroom closet. You and En-ri-que can figure it out shoulder to shoulder." She stretched Enrique's name out like an invitation to something provocative.

Destiny rolled her eyes. "Yeah, yeah. Well, thanks for nothing. I'm so glad I called for all that marvelous help. Looks like I'm stuck here until I can get her moved. She clearly can't live alone. But you knew that, didn't you? Perhaps I can get the neighbor, what was her name, to help."

"Claire Johnson."

"Yes, Mrs. Johnson. She might be able to stay with her long enough for me to check out of the hotel and get my things."

"Her number's on the magnetic white board on the side of the fridge, along with Enrique's business card. Gotta run. Good luck. Talk to you soon. Kiss-kiss."

The line went dead before Destiny could say good-bye. Unbelievable. How could anyone be so oblivious? Still, Angela did fly down there, stay a week with three toddlers. But she wasn't forgiven yet. She should have told Destiny the truth. She couldn't go twenty-four hours without calling in the cavalry. She tiptoed into the kitchen and read the whiteboard. *Claire Johnson 239-555-3478*. Next to it, a white business card, *Enrique Gonzales Lopez, Home Health Aide, Florida Department of Children and Family Services, Medicare/Medicaid 239-555-1200*. In a messy scrawl on the whiteboard, she could barely make out a phone number and Philip's name. As if she'd ever call him.

Below it was a bizarre list.
Month and Year
City where I live
People I love
My name

She dialed Claire's number. "Hello, Mrs. Johnson, this is Captain, I mean, Destiny Osgood, I'm Marlene's daughter." She had to stop that. She wasn't a captain anymore. *It'll take me a while to get used to that.*

"Of course, my dear. Call me Claire. How good of you to call. How is Marlene today? The whole neighborhood's been worried about her."

Destiny could only imagine the gossip, but it was nice to hear a friendly voice. "Claire, would it be too much for you to come and sit with Marlene so I can check out of the Hilton? I guess I'm going to be staying here for now." She looked into the bedroom. Marlene was asleep. Was she feeling empathy for her mother? That was something new. But that didn't mean she forgave her.

"Sure, I'll be right over," said Claire.

Six

After a shower, clean clothes, and minimal make-up, Destiny luxuriated in a five-minute respite on the balcony enjoying the view of the beautiful beach she'd probably never get to walk on. The breeze was wonderful, and she inhaled the smell of salt air. Three pelicans skimmed the surface of the water looking for fish. An osprey flew within ten feet of her, and she watched it land on the railing of the building across the small, impeccable lawn. She patted the arms of the deck chair. It'd be nice to sit here for a while.

When she got back to the condo, Marlene and Claire were sitting at the small dining table, a full breakfast of bacon, eggs, and biscuits in front of them. That woman was a marvel.

Marlene was smartly dressed in white linen slacks and a black silk shirt. And fully made up with mascara and eye shadow.

"Hello," said Claire. "May I call you Destiny? Ready for some breakfast?"

"Yes, thank you." With three cups of coffee sloshing around in Destiny's empty stomach like the waves out in the Gulf, she was more than ready. She slid into the folding chair Claire had magically produced from somewhere. They had to slide the dishes closer together to make room for three at the tiny table. She glanced at Marlene who looked calm and bright-eyed.

"Good morning, Marlene. Don't you look nice this morning. Aren't you lucky to have a friend like Claire who's such a good cook?" Would she remember what had happened earlier with the broken picture frame and the *burglar*?

"Hello, Destiny. Where have you been? Claire's been cooking all day," Marlene said. "I wanted to wait to tell you goodbye before I left."

Destiny glanced over at Claire who only raised an eyebrow. At least Marlene recognized her. That was a start. Forty-five minutes was hardly all day, but Destiny had nothing to gain by bringing that up. No mention of the early morning incident either. That was progress. Perhaps now was a good time to talk to Marlene about her situation, while she was still alert and coherent.

"Are you going somewhere?"

Marlene nodded between bites. "A quick trip across the Alley." A huge smile crossed her lips. "To the Trump Towers."

"The Alley? Trump Towers? Wow. What's that all about?"

Marlene's smile morphed into a grin. "Only a huge commission to paint for The Donald. When I get back, you and I have a lot of catching up to do."

No need to catch up. It had been too long and too much water had passed under the proverbial bridge. There was no reconciliation in their future as far as Destiny was concerned. Once she got Marlene situated, she'd be back on the first plane home to South Carolina. "I brought my things back from the Hilton. I was going to stay here for a few days if that's okay with you. Mar …" Destiny needed to tread lightly. Addressing her as Mom would probably help, but Destiny couldn't spit it out. "Tell me about your work with the J.W. Marriott. Angela says you did all the artwork for their renovations."

Claire placed a steaming plate of bacon and eggs in front of Destiny. It smelled delicious.

Marlene chewed on a fluffy biscuit. She patted her lips with a paper napkin. "Hmm, yes, it was so much fun. You should go there and see them."

Destiny needed answers about the money. "Did it pay well? I don't think I could make a living with my art. I do volunteer work with mine. But you're much more talented than I am." It was the truth, even if Destiny hated to give her mother such an accolade.

"It was a nice commission. Living on commissions is always challenging."

Did that mean she didn't remember or know that she was on disability? Destiny hated prying into her personal business. In reverse shoes, she'd certainly resent it.

Claire gathered the dirty dishes, rinsed them, and dropped them in the dishwasher. "I'm going to head out now. You two don't need me for this little talk."

"Thank you, Claire." Destiny appreciated the discretion. She turned toward her mother. "Um. I ran across some bills that are past due. Do you need some help in that department?"

Mrs. Johnson shot a concerned look at Destiny and quickly exited the condo.

Marlene's blue eyes blazed back at Destiny. "I should say not. I am quite capable of taking care of myself, thank you very much." She huffed and crossed her arms across her chest.

Okay. This wasn't going to be so easy. Destiny shifted in her seat. "I didn't mean to offend you. I'm sure it was an oversight. I could set up your accounts on autopay, so you won't have to worry about them. Do you know where your bank information is?"

Marlene's lips pressed tighter together.

This line of thought was clearly not going to work. Destiny opened her mouth to argue, then thinking better of it, stopped. Her skin prickled with irritation. That familiar feeling nagged in her gut. She was only trying to help. What made her think anything had changed? Marlene didn't love her then, and she didn't love her now.

They moved the few feet into the little living room. Marlene seemed to have forgotten all about the trip across the Alley to meet The Donald. Did she actually have an appointment at Trump Towers? Today, or last week, or last month? Or was it all a delusional fantasy? Destiny admired the artwork on the walls. "Are these like the ones you did for the Marriott?" They were good. Even in black and white, Destiny could envision the colors by the shading of the trees, the water, the sky.

Marlene nodded.

It gave Destiny an idea. She pulled her own charcoal and sketchpad from her bag. "Remember when we used to draw together?" *When I thought you loved me, and we were best pals.* "Want to do it again?"

A smile crossed Marlene's lips, and she nodded again, this time enthusiastically. "We went to the park or to the shore. You were so good with portraits, even as a little one." She looked down at Destiny's left side. "Can you still—"

"Yes, I'm right-handed. Where are your charcoals and sketch pads? I'll get them for you. Would you like to sit outside?"

"In the bottom of the dresser. Left side."

Everything was right where Marlene said it would be. The bottom drawer held dozens of different charcoal sets, colored pencils, acrylics, and oil paints along with sketch pads and canvases of various sizes. And along with the artwork, her checkbook. She questioned her mother's logic but was grateful for the unexpected "gift" of the checkbook. Destiny slipped it into the deep pocket in her skirt and then carried a set of art supplies out to the lanai. Marlene had two easels, so they each set up shop. To keep them cool, Destiny brought glasses of iced tea on a colorful tray she found in the kitchen, and they began to draw in silence.

Marlene's arm swept graceful, delicate strokes across the poster board. She was watching a small sailboat make its way out of the canal. Lost in her art, she was happily oblivious to any problems.

Destiny watched her. As her mother was her only subject, Destiny worked on Marlene's portrait. Destiny's charcoal stick outlined Marlene's high cheekbones and straight nose. She fought the pain that crept into her heart. What had she done to lose her mother's love? She clenched the charcoal in the palm of her hand too tightly, turning it black. *Too hard.* She loosened her grip. *Relax.* Perhaps Marlene was coherent enough to talk. If so, they could talk civilly about her options at the facilities. If she remembered she needed to go there, or if she would even agree. But when Destiny looked back at her face, Marlene was gone. The person she stared at now was not the Marlene of a few moments ago, or the mother of her childhood. This was a bewildered woman, lost in another world. Dark chalk covered her expensive white linen slacks where she was wiping chalk-stained fingers across them. Destiny had missed her chance. Marlene looked back at her easel and continued to draw, but the clear, precise shapes fused into great abstract lines, heavy strokes, the sailboat now nothing but indecipherable scribble.

Marlene turned toward Destiny, zero recognition in her eyes. "Oh, hello. You like to draw too," she stated matter-of-factly. She glanced at the rough sketch of a face on Destiny's pad. "My daughter used to draw portraits too. Do you know her?"

Seven

When Enrique arrived for Marlene's therapy two days later, Destiny headed out, her mother's checkbook in hand. No one had entered anything into the register in months. How was she supposed to balance it with no idea what was coming in or going out? She stepped into the First American Bank of Marco and sought out the manager, the only one with enough authority at the branch to help in her situation. *If* they could help. She wasn't a co-signer on her mother's account.

She headed directly to the office enclosed in glass. Destiny read the name badge pinned to the tan wrap-around dress of the young lady sitting at the desk: Natalie Jensen, Assistant Branch Manager. "Miss Jensen? Ma'am? My name is Cap—err … Destiny Osgood. My mother, Marlene Osgood, is a customer of yours. May I speak with you concerning her account?"

Miss Jensen, petite and much younger than Destiny, offered a wan smile and invited her to sit.

Destiny took a seat in front of the desk and presented the checkbook. "Unfortunately, my mother has developed early onset Alzheimer's disease. I'm here taking care of her." Is that what she was doing? "I noticed that several of her bills are past due. Is it possible to set up some auto-pays from her checking account to cover things like utilities, condo fees, and so forth? I'm afraid she hasn't recorded anything in this check register in a long time, so I have no idea how much is in there."

Miss Jensen typed the account numbers into her PC. The corners of her mouth turned down. "Miss Osgood."

Destiny fought the urge to correct her to Captain Osgood. But she wasn't a captain anymore. She was a civilian. When would she get used to that?

Natalie Jensen's brows furrowed together. Another eighth of an inch and she'd have a unibrow. "Do you have a Power of Attorney for her affairs? Are you her primary care giver? Your mother is the only name listed on her account. I can't give you any information unless she comes in and signs a form adding you to her account. Privacy laws, you know." She slid the checkbook back across the desk.

Destiny was not going to be dismissed that easily. "Ma'am, I do not have a Power of Attorney, and yes, I guess at least temporarily I am her primary care giver. But aren't there times when it's prudent to bend the rules? I'm not asking for access to her cash. I simply want to set up payments directly to her creditors. My mother is in no condition to come in and sign anything."

Miss Jensen studied the screen. "She's well enough to withdraw cash from the ATM on a regular basis. Perhaps you should speak to her about that."

Cash withdrawals? No way Marlene could be doing that. From what she gathered from Angela, Marlene hadn't left the house in months except to go to doctors' appointments and the hairdresser. If she wasn't taking the money out, then who was?

"That doesn't sound possible knowing her health. Do you have cameras on your ATM machines? I suspect someone other than my mother is using her debit card. Can you at least put a stop or fraud alert on her card until we straighten this out?"

Natalie Jenson batted her heavily made-up cobalt blue lashes and shot Destiny a superior, know-it-all look. "If you were her court appointed guardian or had Power of Attorney, then we could investigate further, and you could be added to the account and you could set up the auto bill pay, but until then ..." Her voice trailed off.

Destiny felt her blood pressure spike. Breathe in, two, three, four, hold, two three four, and out, two, three, four. She'd accomplish nothing by losing her temper. Approach the enemy with tact and restraint. "And how would I go about that?"

"An attorney can draw up the papers for you. A doctor would have to attest to the fact that Mrs. Osgood can't handle her own affairs. Then, you'd need to have it recorded with the courts." She stood and extended her hand, dismissing Destiny. "Once we have the legal documentation, we'll be glad to assist you."

Destiny followed suit, stood, and gripped Ms. Jenson's hand, a tad too tightly. "Ma'am, it's been a pleasure," she said through gritted teeth. At least she had a plan. She turned on her heel and left. She hoped Little Miss Priss caught her sarcasm.

For a half a second, Destiny contemplated signing her mother's name on her checks. With her luck, someone would recognize the change in signature, and she'd be arrested for fraud. And what if there wasn't enough money in the account to cover the checks? No, she couldn't do that. She still had no idea of the balance in the account. With no other imminent options, she'd have to use her own funds to pay Marlene's bills and buy the groceries or hit Angela up for it. It was only temporary. It was a good thing she hadn't had much opportunity to spend her pay in Afghanistan. Most of her money, little as it was, had gone into a savings account back home.

Destiny pulled into the Publix grocery store parking lot and glared at the ATM machine attached to the side of the building by the entrance. Who was using Marlene's card? Did she leave her card someplace and an unscrupulous person picked it up, or did she give it to someone to pick things up for her? Was Destiny overreacting? It could all be legitimate and with Marlene's consent. Destiny's gut told her that was unlikely.

If the card was also a credit card, it would be easy for someone to sign her name. Most cashiers rarely checked to match a name on a card. God only knows how many things were paid for on her card on top of the cash withdrawals. Possibly someone gave her a ride to the bank at one time and kept the card. Marlene wouldn't remember now.

What about Enrique? Would he do something like that? Was he short on cash? How much did home health aides employed by the state make? It couldn't be much. He'd certainly have the opportunity if he ever took her out. She'd read about things like that: people posing as helpers and ripping off the elderly and infirm left and right. She hadn't asked for identification. What if he wasn't even an aide? Anyone could have business cards made up. She would have to do more investigating. She mentally chastised herself. What did it matter if it was him? Still, it felt like an appalling betrayal. Destiny hoped it wasn't him.

And what about this Philip guy? She'd have to meet him soon and check him out too. This was another complication she didn't need. Destiny rubbed the back of her neck. She tried to hurry through the aisles, but senior citizens thought nothing of blocking the aisles with their riding grocery carts or walkers while they exchanged the latest news about someone's newest hip or latest infirmity. Duly noted to choose a time less crowded with seniors, if there was such a time. Perhaps midnight? She looked around. Were there any young people on this island? After buying essentials, Destiny headed back to the condo.

She'd have to approach the subject of the cash withdrawals delicately. Destiny didn't know for a fact that money was being stolen. Could she possibly be lucky enough to have Marlene lucid and with a simple explanation for it all?

Eight

At the condo, Marlene was dressed, sitting in her chair by the sliding glass doors in her bedroom. Enrique was talking to her about hygiene. On a folding TV tray, he had a hairbrush, a toothbrush and paste, and a solid stick of deodorant. Her mission, should she choose to accept it, was to tell him what each object was for and how to use them.

Destiny didn't interrupt and busied herself with the groceries.

"Try again, Marlene," she heard Enrique say. "That's toothpaste. You use it to clean your teeth."

Looking around the corner, Destiny saw him gently wiping toothpaste from Marlene's cheek. She must have thought it was foundation or powder. For a brief second, Destiny felt a rush of satisfaction— like her mother deserved this. Oh God, she didn't believe that did she? Of course not.

Enrique and Marlene looked up as Destiny entered the bedroom. His face lit up. Marlene's clouded over.

"Groceries all put away," Destiny said. "How's it going here?"

Enrique gathered the items off the tray and put them away where they belonged. "Miss Marlene's having a little trouble with her short-term memory today. But we're not giving up, are we?" When Marlene didn't answer, he flung his backpack over one shoulder. "See you on Tuesday, Miss Marlene." He nodded. "Miss Destiny."

"It's Destiny, just Destiny."

Destiny watched Marlene pick up a sneaker from beside her chair and rip the Velcro off and on repeatedly. Her hands showed the beginning of wrinkles. They once drew such beautiful pictures. Would they ever again? Seeing this obsessive compulsion twisted Destiny's gut. What a horrid disease, this early onset Alzheimer's. On the outside, Marlene didn't look any different than any other middle-aged woman. But on the inside, she was old, withering away. Destiny picked up Marlene's sketch pad and offered a charcoal stick in replacement for the shoe. Marlene hesitated for a minute, then she smiled and accepted the stick. It was nothing short of miraculous to see the physical change to her face when her mind brought her back to the present.

"Thank you. I haven't drawn in such a very long time."

Apparently, she'd forgotten her last attempt that ended in the wild scribblings. Just as well. Here was a rare window into her present mind.

Destiny couldn't let these precious moments slip by without getting answers. "Marlene, do you know who your family doctor is? Or where his office is?"

"Of course," she said nonchalantly. "Dan Goldstein has been my doctor ever since I moved to the island. His office is right across from City Hall."

Enrique stopped in the doorway to smile at Marlene's sudden alertness. "Right, Marlene. Good job."

"Yes," said Destiny. "I'd like to meet him. Is it all right if I call and make an appointment? Perhaps he could take a look at you at the same time." She glanced over Marlene's shoulder. She was sketching the mango tree and the tall Royal palms down by the docks. Her touch was delicate and precise.

Destiny felt a tug at her heart as a memory flashed before her. They were sitting together on a big rock by the shore at Myrtle Beach. Destiny had been about eight years old. It was a beautiful summer evening. Her mom was beautiful and wore bright yellow capris and a gauzy white blouse. Her bright pink toenails peeked through the sand. Her flaxen hair was long, and the wind caught it and twirled it around her head like a halo. She was drawing the sunset. Destiny was sketching, and three-year-old Angela was playing in the sand.

A lump in Destiny's throat kept her from speaking when suddenly, instead of Angela tossing beach sand in the air, desert sand whipped around her as the swirling blades of a Boeing CH-47D Chinook helicopter spun out of control as it was hit by a mortar. Everything exploded in front of her eyes. Metal, body parts, and blood filled her vision. It had killed eighteen of America's finest treasures. Destiny shook off the image and practiced a few breathing exercises to bring her heart rate back down.

"Are you all right?" Enrique asked.

Destiny had forgotten he was still there. "Yes, yes, thank you. Do you happen to know Dr. Goldstein's number?"

"Of course." He set his bag down and headed for the white board in the kitchen.

Marlene glanced at Destiny. "You were always such a rambunctious child. The only way we could get you to sit still was to put a sketch pad in front of you. Do you still draw, Destiny?"

"You mean since you walked out on me?" asked Destiny.

Enrique's head swung around to look at her.

Damn. Did she say that out loud? She swallowed the rock lodged in her throat.

If Marlene had heard her comment, there was no reaction.

Destiny started over. "Yes, I always have my charcoal and pads with me. I work with the Wounded Warrior project on the base using art as therapy for their PTSD." She knelt and reached for her rucksack in the living room, pulling out her charcoals. But she didn't want to bond with Marlene now. She wanted answers.

"Frank?" Marlene suddenly called out in a sing-song voice. "Angela is crying. Can you pick her up? I can't handle both of them."

Whoa. Destiny watched the muscles in Marlene's face change. The light was gone from her mother's eyes, the reality vanished. She actually looked younger, like a young mother. Was that for real? How would Destiny know if she was acting? Too bizarre. The reality punched Destiny's gut. Marlene couldn't handle both her and Angela, so she had to choose one. Tag, you're it, Angela.

Destiny pulled herself off wobbly knees and made it to the kitchen. What was she thinking coming here? The visit was a constant reminder of the past, the wound that would never heal. She needed more than water now. The wine bottle from dinner the other night was empty. *Was there any alcohol in this place?* If only she'd stopped at a liquor store.

Enrique pointed to the white board. "I wrote Dr. Goldstein's number on the board for you." He stared down at his feet. "I'm sorry. I didn't mean to eavesdrop or to pry, but I couldn't help but hear your comment about her walking out on you. Did your parents split up when you were little?"

Destiny shrugged. "It's okay. Old baggage. Sorry for my outburst. Was there something else you needed?" She didn't want to talk about it, especially with him. Back to her mission.

"Nothing too important. I wanted to remind you to make sure she takes her medications, the Aricept, the Namenda, and the vitamins. They help with her cognitive abilities. I'll be back day after tomorrow."

Destiny nodded. Now was as good a time as any. "Enrique, do you know who usually takes Marlene to her doctor's appointments?"

"Sometimes I take her. But if her appointment isn't on one of my scheduled days, Mrs. Johnson takes her. Your sister took her last week. Philip may have taken her a few times. And before that, she drove herself. Angela hid the car keys from her when she was here."

"Did you make other stops when you drove her, like at the pharmacy or bank?" *Please say no.* She shook off the feeling. Why should she care?

He flashed her a toothy smile. God, that smile. "Sometimes. Miss Marlene liked to stop at the Cold Stone Creamery at the Esplanade. That lady loves her ice cream."

Destiny never knew her mother loved ice cream. She had no recollection of Marlene ever wanting it when she was a child. There were dozens of things Destiny didn't know about Marlene. Or her about Destiny. And whose fault was that? Marlene chose someone over Destiny. And there it was, the pity party, like a broken record. She had to stop. Why couldn't she let it go? She was an adult, a soldier. In her mind, she knew it was illogical and immature. So, her parents split up. Big deal. Single parents raise lots of kids. The colonel was a good father, the best, in fact. She'd turned out okay, hadn't she? But the familiar pain shot through her heart, an actual physical pain as if her heart was breaking.

"What about other people that have been here to visit my mother? Any idea who that would be?"

Enrique stepped out into the blast of humid Florida air. "Besides Philip? Not sure you'd call it a visit, but she has a cleaning lady every two weeks, and I think she had the A/C man here before Angela got here. Why?"

Destiny stepped toward him. "Well, there's a situation."

He waited, hand on the doorknob.

"Someone's been making cash withdrawals from Marlene's checking account. I can't imagine that it could be her. Do you happen to know where her debit card is?"

Enrique's face darkened and he pointed at his chest. "Are you accusing me of taking Miss Marlene's money?"

"No, no," Destiny backpedaled. "I'm afraid she dropped it somewhere, and a stranger has it. They won't give me any details at the bank until I become an authorized user on her account—which of course, is fraught with red tape. Do you think the cleaning lady or the A/C guy could possibly have taken it? Did she pay them with a credit card? Or what about Philip?"

"Philip, yeah, I could see him doing that, but I suppose I am a little prejudiced against him. I don't have any real reason to suspect him. I don't like him. I wasn't here when the A/C guy was here, but I saw Angela pay the cleaning lady with cash. No idea before Angela was here."

"Hmm. Could you help me look around the apartment to see if we can find it? If not, I'll have to report it as stolen."

His shoulders relaxed. He stepped back through the threshold and closed the door behind him. Setting his backpack on the counter, "Of course. Have you looked in her purse?"

"Naturally. That was the first place I looked. Not there. But people with dementia put things in strange places, don't they? Either she's withdrawing the cash with someone's help or someone close to her is taking cash without her knowledge and putting the card back. And if the card can't be found? Then it's lost or stolen."

Together they scoured the apartment. It felt so intrusive going through Marlene's drawers. They even searched under the mattress and in the refrigerator. Nothing.

"Sorry," Enrique said. "It wasn't me. I hope you believe that."

Destiny offered a tired smile. "I do. Thanks for helping." She did believe him, didn't she?

She sat alone at the dining table. Now what? It didn't entirely put Enrique in the clear, but it didn't make him the culprit either. She fostered a sigh of relief. She'd ask Claire Johnson if she had the air conditioner company's name or the name of the cleaning lady. And then there was Philip.

Enrique stuck his head back through the door. "Um, Miss Destiny? Would you like to go out sometime, like for coffee or something?" He ducked his head, looking sheepish.

As in a date? Destiny stood and faced him. "Again, please drop the Miss. I'm Destiny. First, I can hardly leave Marlene alone, as you well know." She waved her good hand around the little condo. "And second, thank you, but I don't date."

"Never?" Enrique raised one eyebrow and his eyes danced. "Did I *say* it was a date?"

Of course not. Why would a hunk like that want to date her? She tucked her arm behind her back. Destiny shook her head. "Not really. Sorry if I misunderstood. I'm a little overwhelmed at the moment."

He winked. "I didn't say it *wouldn't* be a date. It *could* be, if you wanted it to be."

Oh, no. She didn't need this. Did he have some sick fascination with the maimed and homely? "Well, that's still a no. I want to get Marlene settled somewhere safe so I can get out of here."

"O-k-a-y." Enrique raised his hands in surrender. "Whatever you say." He lowered his head and made his second exit.

Claire joined Destiny at the table for a pot of tea the next day. Marlene was sitting in her slipper chair, staring out at the water. Destiny couldn't tell whether she was coherent or in another reality. It was good to have some time alone with Claire.

"Claire, you wouldn't happen to know what happened to Marlene's debit card, would you? I can't put my finger on it. Honestly, it's a wonder we can find anything around here with the strange places she puts things these days. The day I got here, there was an umbrella hanging from the chandelier." Destiny hoped she did not come off accusatory, like she had with Enrique.

Claire chuckled and scooped another heaping teaspoon of sugar into her cup. That woman sure had a sweet tooth. "I know. I always try to put things back in order when I am here. But then, she does something like that again. As for her credit card, I think

I saw her give it to the receptionist at the doctor's office the last time I accompanied her."

Destiny nodded. "Oh, that must be it. We've hunted high and low for it. We even looked in the refrigerator."

Claire cackled, reminding Destiny of the Afghan women that hooted in large groups in the middle of ruins in ancient buildings bombed to rubble. Claire went into a story of finding her cell phone in the linen closet one time. "Getting old is hell, Alzheimer's or not."

"Enrique told me Marlene has a cleaning lady. And that the A/C guy was recently here. Would you happen to know how I can contact them? Perhaps one of them mistakenly picked up her card when she was paying them."

"I think it was Cooper Air Conditioning. I had them service my A/C while they were here. I have their card at my place. I'll bring it over for you. The cleaning lady's name is Maria, but that's all I know. Must be a thousand cleaning ladies with that name around here."

"True. Does she still come? Do you know what days? And that would be great if I could have the card for the A/C company."

"I haven't seen Maria since before Angela was here. Maybe Angela would know."

Destiny phoned Dr. Goldstein's office. His receptionist, a pleasant voice who answered to Helen, made an appointment for Marlene for the following

Thursday and scheduled some extra time for the doctor to speak to Destiny in private.

"Helen, by any chance, did my mother leave her credit card last time she was there?"

"Oh, no. If one was left here, we would have notified her immediately."

Wasn't giving information to a patient with Alzheimer's an unwise decision? When she spoke to the doctor in person, she'd ask for the affidavit for the attorney to bring to the bank. She remembered the short to-do list she scribbled on her way here and snickered at her own naivety. Yeah, right. As if it would've been that easy. And besides, when did life ever serve her *easy*?

Nine

Marlene

They think I don't know that something's wrong, but I do. I should know these people, but I don't. The faces are familiar but remain unrecognizable, as if I can't unlock the answer from my mind. I concentrate, close my eyes, and dig into my memory, but nothing. Are they friend or foe? Should I act happy to see them or scream for help?

And this place—where am I? Where's my house, Frank, the girls? I look down at my body, and my heart sinks at what I see. Hands aged with time, a roundness to my middle I never knew I had. When had that happened? Am I old now? Is this a nightmare? Will I wake up, and everything go back to normal?

My lips are trembling, so I press my fingers to them, trying to hold back the tears that threaten to fall. It's terrifying, and I have no one to tell, no one I know. So, I throw things against the wall. I scream in frustration.

People come and go from my peripheral vision, always pleasant, but treating me like a child, speaking slowly, a little too loud, keeping sentences short. I want to tell them all to go away, to leave me alone, let me figure this out.

The one that calls herself Destiny bewilders me the most. Is this my little Dezi, all grown up? She's missing a hand and part of her arm. I can see through her blouse where her upper arm joins the artificial thingy. What happened to her? Looking at her facial features, that strong chin, the dark hair; it could be her. She looks a lot like Frank. Why would she say she was Dezi if she wasn't? Has she forgiven me? Sometimes mistakes you make can be chalked up as lessons learned in life. But others, like in this case, alter your life and that of everyone around you forever.

Sleep forces my eyes to close. I hate sleep. Once I loved sleep, when the girls were little, and I could grab a cat nap wherever I could. Not now. Where would I be when I woke up?

A man comes into my room. He startles me, calls me "Miss Marlene." A nice-looking young man, but I have no idea who he is. Should I be afraid? He certainly acts like he's supposed to be here. He sets things on a table and asks me to name them. What kind of test is that? And who is he to be asking that of me? Kind of rude, in my opinion. I cross my arms and refuse to participate in his silly games. Between you, me and the lamppost, there are some things I can't name. That thing you pull through your hair to make it smooth. I know what to do with it. Why can't I name it? *Phft*, what difference does it make as long as I know what to use it for?

I watch the girl calling herself Destiny and him. Enrique—that's it, I think. What kind of name is that? Kind of, shoot, what's that word? Oh, yeah, exotic. And yes, he is exotic looking. Destiny thinks so, too, I can tell. I see a sparkle in her eyes when she looks at him. There is something going on between those two, even if they don't think I know.

This not knowing stuff is driving me crazy. I must do something about it. Lists. I've always been good with lists. If I could find my planner, I'd write things down as they happen, people's names, and names of things when they come to me. I look down at the bracelet on wrist. Run my fingers over the words. *Memory Impaired. Call 9-1-1.* My breath catches. I really am losing my memory. And I'm the only one that can slow it down.

"Destiny, may I ask you a favor?"

The girl called Destiny looks up. She seems pleased that I know her name.

"Of course, what is it?"

"May I have my, *what is that word? ... planner, yes that's it*, planner, so I can write things down? I can make lists to help me remember things." I sit back, pleased at myself for remembering the word.

"What a great idea. I think I saw one in your nightstand. Let me get it for you."

This woman looks a lot like I'd expect my Destiny to look when she grew up. But somehow not quite. Harder somehow and broken. But how could she not be if she had a terrible accident and lost her arm? I see pain in her eyes sometimes.

She finds the planner and hands it to me. Most of it is blank, but as I flip through, I see dates and names. I need to use it more. I wish I'd thought of this sooner.

Ten

Thursday started off better than expected. Marlene was clear as a bell and pleasant. She seemed genuinely pleased to be seeing Dr. Goldstein. After a good breakfast that she ate without difficulty, she dressed herself. Only her color choices of white capris with pink flamingos and a lime green top momentarily made Destiny question her clarity. But when she pulled a pink and lime green cloth handbag from the closet, Destiny realized her choices were deliberate. In contrast, Destiny's khaki chinos and white T-shirt looked drab and out of place in this floral, tropical world.

Dr. Goldstein's office was cheery, with soft cushioned chairs in green palm-frond prints that matched the green-framed paintings on the walls. Her mother's drawings. Destiny's mouth dropped open in awe. Were Marlene's paintings all over the island? There were six of them, evenly spaced above the chairs that backed the wall. She paused in front of each one and admired the amazingly detailed work. When had Marlene done these? Was this further proof of her success as an artist? Destiny didn't give Marlene enough credit.

"Wow, you made these, didn't you?" Destiny smiled at her mother. "Are you some kind of local celebrity artist? I'm impressed."

Marlene didn't look up at her handiwork or acknowledge her question but delved into a deep conversation with a lady with heavy elastic stockings about varicose veins. Thirty minutes after their scheduled appointment time, a nurse ushered them into an exam room. After the normal checks of blood pressure, pulse, and temperature by a nurse's assistant, all normal, Dr. Goldstein knocked lightly on the door and entered.

"Marlene, you're looking well. Good numbers here." He nodded, tapping on his iPad. Destiny assumed they were the results the assistant obtained.

"I'm good, Doctor Dan," Marlene smiled at him. "This is my daughter, Destiny. She's here for a visit with me. Unexpected, but nice."

Doctor Dan was only about ten years older than Destiny, nice-looking, without being too gorgeous for her to be naked under a sheet in front of him. He had that no-nonsense, get-things-done set to his strong chin. Perhaps he would have some answers about Marlene's prognosis. His gaze assessed Destiny's mechanical hand, but he said nothing as he reached for her other hand to shake.

He ran Marlene through a set of cognitive tests, her name, address, name of the President, what year it was. She passed them all with flying colors. He sat beside her and talked casually, but she interrupted to introduce Destiny again. Doctor Dan went through the introduction as if it was the first time, then continued with his questions. She struggled with her sister's name and kept asking where her father was.

"Marlene, can you say the alphabet backwards, starting with Z?" asked the doctor.

Destiny mentally tried to do it. Not an easy feat without intense concentration. That hardly seemed like a fair test.

"Z … Y … W." Marlene stalled, them burst out in raw laughter. "I can't even do it forward without singing the alphabet song in my head. And I still get stuck on L, M, N, O, P when I'm filing. Trust me, you'd never want me as your file clerk."

Doctor Dan chuckled. "Fair enough."

Destiny sang the Alphabet song silently in her head. *A, B, C, D, E, F, G …* ending with *Now I know my ABC's, next time won't you sing with me.*

"May I speak to Destiny for a few minutes alone, Marlene? We need to discuss some private stuff."

"Of course, Patrick. I'll wait out in the other room."

Patrick? What happened to Doctor Dan? Without batting an eye, he ushered her to the lobby, and she struck up a conversation with an elderly gentleman. Then he and Destiny stepped into his office, and he closed the door.

"What's going on, doctor? As you can see, sometimes she is perfectly rational and others …"

He nodded. "I'm afraid she's quickly moving into stage six of the disease. She'll recognize less and less in the coming weeks. And don't be surprised if she gets hostile."

Whoa. Hostile? Stage Six? What did all that mean? Destiny's temples began to pound against her skull. Her legs suddenly felt rubbery, and she sank into a chair across from his large mahogany desk.

The doctor offered her a paper cup of water.

"Thank you," she mumbled, grateful to quench her suddenly dry mouth.

"I know this is a lot to take in all at once. But your mother has had this disease much longer than you suspect. Many people go through the first several stages without a clear diagnosis, especially if they are up in years. But with your mother's younger age and her cognitive problems, it alerted us that something was out of the ordinary. Early onset Alzheimer's only applies to about 5% of Alzheimer's patients, the ones diagnosed before the age of sixty-five. I've been monitoring your mother for quite some time."

Destiny sipped at the last drop of water and crushed the empty cup in her fist. Did Angela know all this time? Destiny was wrong to expect Angela to carry this burden by herself because of Destiny's personal issues with their mother. This was both of their problems, not only Angela's. Destiny shivered. When had she ever been there for Angela? Never. When she was growing up, Destiny treated Angela not much differently than she treated Marlene, giving lip service to a long-distance relationship that didn't actually exist. And after the Colonel, their dad, died, Destiny's feeble efforts to be the good big sister now looked charged with self-righteousness. If she was honest with herself, she resented Angela for being the chosen child, the one Marlene chose to go with her when she left. Destiny tried to tell herself that was ridiculous. Angela had no control over the situation. But it still made it hard to be the big sister she should have been.

"So, she'll be needing permanent long-term care." Dr. Goldstein said.

His words drew Destiny back to the present. "Excuse me. You were saying?"

Dr. Goldstein cleared his throat, his eyes boring into her. "That she will soon be needing full-time long-term care. Angela made arrangements for Marlene at a wonderful facility, but there's a waiting list." His eyes narrowed and met hers. "She told me that you didn't have the best relationship with your mother."

That was the understatement of the century. Destiny came here anxious to throw her mother away and forget about her. She hadn't given Marlene or Angela much thought in years. Destiny shook her head. *I'm acting like a narcissistic pig. This isn't about me, not even my abandonment by this woman.* It was time to shift gears. She needed to think about what was best for Marlene and Angela, not herself.

"Correct. But I'm here now, aren't I?" She straightened in her chair. "Right now, I'm trying to figure out her finances. Who's paying for the home health aide? And your fees?"

He studied Destiny for a minute without answering. What did he see when he looked at her? From his knowledge of the relationship, probably not much. Most likely the exact person she came here planning to be. Someone she was not proud of.

He readjusted his glasses and read the notes in the file on his desk. "For now, Marlene is still covered with Medicaid through her Social Security Disability. She qualified for home health services through the Florida Children and Families Services. But there is a limit on the number of occupational sessions she can have. So, unless she has some other supplemental insurance that we don't know about, I'm afraid her sessions with her Home Health aide will stop in another two weeks. And to be honest, as rapidly as this is progressing, she will most likely hit stage seven fairly quickly, and therapy will be futile."

A feeling of dread settled in Destiny's stomach. "Stage seven? What does that mean?"

"Miss Osgood, or Destiny, if I may, there are seven stages to Alzheimer's Disease, and every case is different."

Destiny shrugged. "Destiny is fine."

Dr. Goldstein nodded and continued. "But the progression is the same, although the timeframe often differs. Your mother is declining far more rapidly than people who acquire Alzheimer's in their later years. The fatality rate in early onset is very high."

"Are you telling me that she's dying?" What had she expected? That Marlene would lose her memory and live in a fairy-tale bliss until old age? But die? Not at fifty-five. Women her age didn't die — not unless it was breast cancer or a car accident. Not from dementia. She glanced over at the closed door between his office and the waiting room, where Marlene sat totally unaware of the fate awaiting her. "Does she know?"

Dr. Goldstein shook his head. "She was told the prognosis by the neurologist when she was first diagnosed. But she probably can't remember or won't shortly. It's confusing enough for patients with early onset to deal with the memory lapses. They know that they don't know something, but they can't put their finger on exactly what it is. That can frustrate them, so they act out." He tapped a pen on his desk, watching it make small dots on his blotter. "It's a lot like the men and women that came back from war, scarred and damaged, whether inside or out." His eyes traveled to her left side.

Destiny shifted in her seat, covering her mechanical hand with her purse. Was he seeing something in her? Was her PTSD showing?

She gulped. "I understand that. I'm an assistant art therapist with the Wounded Warrior Project. I got my degree online while I was on active duty and was waiting for my accreditation before I left for the Middle East. I plan to complete it now that I'm home." She caught herself from rambling. Why was she going into all this detail? He didn't care. She wasn't the patient here.

Dr. Goldstein's eyes met hers. He was trying to tell her about Marlene, and she was babbling about her own issues. "If I had to put a time frame on it," he continued, "I'd give her another year at the most. I'm so sorry. Most likely, she won't recognize you, at least not as an adult, within six months. She'll progress backwards, getting younger and younger in her mind. Best to go along with her. You'll probably see her as a young mother, then a teenager, even a child. When she reaches stage seven, she'll be like an infant, then she'll forget to swallow, forget to chew, have no control over her bowels. It's never a pretty sight. I wish I had better news."

Wow. That hardly seemed possible. Destiny wished she'd kept that cup. She could have used some more water. A vision of soldiers dying right before her eyes. Of Max dying. She saw the fear in his eyes, the pleading to save him. It was a blessing that Marlene didn't know. She swallowed hard. She was a soldier. She'd seen people die before. She could handle this, couldn't she?

They talked briefly about long-term care, and Dr. Goldstein explained that Destiny wouldn't be able to care for her mother soon. It would be difficult in stage six and impossible in stage seven. "I hate to sound so doomsday. It's entirely possible that she could stay at this stage for a year or two. I've been wrong before. We don't have all the answers. That's why they call it practicing medicine." He was throwing her a lifeline, a flicker of hope.

Destiny raised her head and met his gaze square in the eyes. "But you don't actually think so, do you?"

His head barely rocked from side to side, and he looked down at the papers on his desk again. "One more thing, Destiny. Research shows that those who have a parent or sibling with Alzheimer's are more likely to develop the disease than those who do not have a first-degree relative with Alzheimer's. There is a molecular genetic test that could show if you carry the gene. Would you like to be tested?" Destiny thought of Angela and her children. Had she passed the gene on to her children? She shook her head. "Uh, no. At least not right now. Was Angela tested?"

"I don't know. I gave her the same information, but she was going to discuss it with her husband, and if she wanted to be tested, she would have it done in San Diego."

Destiny had temporarily forgotten why she'd asked for the private meeting in the first place. *Oh, yeah.* The money.

The doctor went on to explain that long term care could run as much as $7000 a month. She did a quick calculation. *Crap.* That was eighty grand a year. Did Marlene or even Sam have that kind of money? Destiny sure didn't in her meager savings.

"I need an affidavit or Power of Attorney from you so the bank will make me her financial custodian. As you know, she can't perform basic banking anymore. Can you handle that for me?"

"Of course." The doctor tapped something into his tablet. "The front desk will have it for you when you leave."

Destiny forced herself out of the chair and extended her hand. "Thank you for your frankness, Dr. Goldstein." She retrieved the paperwork from the front desk, steered Marlene by the arm, and accompanied her home.

If Marlene was aware that this had not been a clean health report, she didn't let on. She chatted in the car about playing a recent game of mahjong with her friends. Destiny knew for a fact from Claire that she hadn't been to a game in months. Perhaps

Marlene was the lucky one, totally unaware of what was going on in her own brain.

As they proceeded up the walk, Destiny noticed a different car in Marlene's assigned spot. An old Chevy Impala. It had to be at least thirty years old. The body was half-covered in Bondo, had not been repainted in several places, and the bumpers were more rust than metal. She couldn't even tell what color it was supposed to be. "Mar … who's car is that?"

Marlene's face lit up at the sight of it. "Oh, that's Philip's."

Wonderful. At least Destiny would get a chance to check him out. "How did he get in your house if you weren't home?"

"He has a key of course. I'm so excited for you to meet him."

When Destiny opened the door, she had to stifle a laugh. Was this guy for real? He was sprawled across the small sofa, his hairy legs and dirty bare feet hanging off the end. Sound asleep. He wore his stringy light brown hair pulled into a thin ponytail at the nape of his neck. A three-day shadow covered his cheeks, one of which was pressed into a decorator pillow. He wore a wrinkled Hawaiian shirt above khaki cargo shorts.

Marlene went over to Prince Philip and jiggled his shoulder. "Philip, wake up. We've got company."

He grumbled and swatted her hand away, burrowing down deeper into the pillow.

"He had to perform last night," Marlene offered as an explanation. "The poor man works too many late hours." She turned to Destiny. "He's a singer at the J.W. He's quite talented."

Somehow, Destiny doubted that. She whispered. "What should we do with him?"

"Nothing. Let him sleep it off. I could use a little nap myself. You can run along if you like. I'm fine here with Philip."

Run along where? She had checked out of the hotel, and she didn't feel a bit comfortable with this man in her mother's house. "I'll stick around here if that's okay with you. I'll make myself some coffee and read a book at the kitchen table while he sleeps."

"Suit yourself," said Marlene. "I'll be in my room."

At least Destiny had the affidavit from the doctor, and she could straighten out her bank issues as soon as she found an attorney to file it with the court. She made coffee, sat it on the small table, and called Angela. The guilt for leaving all this on Angela scratched at her conscience. Sister-of-the-year Destiny was not.

Angela picked up on the first ring.

"Ange, why didn't you tell me?" Destiny whispered into the phone.

"Hello to you, too," Angela replied. "And why are you whispering? Tell you what?"

"Philip is here. Asleep on the couch. We went to see Dr. Goldstein today. He told me the prognosis. And he led me to believe that you've known about Marlene's condition for some time. Is that true?"

Destiny heard pots or pans banging in the background, then shuffling and shooing.

Angela gave a slight laugh. "Sorry, the kids are into everything today. I pulled the twins out from under the cabinets. Their favorite toys this week are pots and pans."

"Ange, what about Mom?" Did she say Mom? Without even thinking?

"We've been through this, Dezi. You didn't want to know. Remember? Are you getting soft on Mom now that she's sick?"

"Sick? She's not sick," Destiny hissed. "She's dying. Don't you think I had a right to know?"

A big sigh came through the speaker. "That's why I sent for you. You had to see it for yourself. That and I couldn't stay there with three toddlers. Well, now you know. Does that mean you are finally going to forgive her?"

A familiar prickliness crept up Destiny's back. Now, *she* was the bad guy? "I wasn't the one that left, remember? She left me. And it looks like she's going to leave me again, permanently." As quickly as the anger crept in, it blew away like the breeze from the Gulf. "I'm sorry. That was unnecessary. I'm glad I called you so I should share this responsibility."

"If you could only find it in your heart to forgive her." Angela shouted into the phone over the banging in the background. "Don't you think you owe her that much—a chance to explain before you let her die with a broken heart? She's tried for years to talk to you, but you wouldn't hear it."

Rather than answering, Destiny changed the subject. She wasn't ready to get into that now, if ever. "Ange, there's more. Dr. Goldstein said that

Alzheimer's may be genetic. Are you worried about your kids? Have you been tested?"

Thankfully, the banging finally ended at Angela's end. The little darlings must have moved on to other mischief. At least toddlers had short attention spans.

Angela's voice returned to normal volume. "I was worried, so I did get tested. I'm good. I don't have the gene. Are you going to get tested?"

"Well, since I don't even have a man on the horizon, I'm not going to be passing it down to any kids, so I don't have to worry about that, at least not now."

Angela laughed. "What about Enrique? Are things heating up on that front?"

Only in my dreams. "Please. I have enough on my plate. I don't need a man in my life. I'm not sure I trust Enrique or Mr. Prince Philip here on the couch. Either one could be after her money."

"What money? Do you know something I don't?" asked Angela.

"No, but they both seem a little too friendly for my liking." She glanced at Philip who let out a loud snore. "Speaking of Prince Philip, what am I supposed to do with this man on Mom's couch? She can't love this guy, can she?"

"I don't know. She says they've been together for years. Thank God, he doesn't live there full time. He seems to come and go at his own will. As for Enrique, I totally trust him. He's a very compassionate man. I'm sure the Florida Children and Family Services would have vetted him before they sent him out on house calls."

"Well, we'll see." Destiny lowered her voice even more. "And as for this Philip guy, I don't like him, and I haven't even spoken to him yet."

"Trust me, Dezi, it won't get any better when you do."

Philip rolled over and sat up, rubbing his eyes.

"He's awake. Gotta go." Destiny hung up.

Philip's eyes narrowed when he noticed Destiny sitting at the small dining room table. "Who are you?"

"Marlene's daughter, Destiny." She stood and walked two steps toward him. "And you are?"

"Philip. Marlene's boyfriend. What are you doing here?" It was more of an accusation than an innocent question. His eyes traveled up and down her and landed on her breasts. Well, that was a switch. At least it wasn't her prosthetic.

"I guess I could be asking you the same thing. Why don't we start over? I'm not here to bust your chops, and I'd like to get out of here as fast as you probably want me gone. But the truth is, Marlene is sick. And I guess it's my duty to make sure she's taken care of."

He belched and waved a hand in front of his face. "I'm taking care of her. You can leave anytime."

Destiny felt the hairs on the back of her neck stand up. "Really? I've been here over a week, and this is the first I have seen or heard from you. How is that taking care of her?"

"She's fine. You, your little sister, and that Mexican dude have got this thing blown way out of proportion. So, she forgets things sometimes. We all do, even you, I'd bet."

Destiny lowered her voice and spoke slowly. "Listen, Philip. We just came from her doctor's office. She doesn't simply forget things. She has Alzheimer's disease, and she is dying. If you cared one hoot, you would have known that."

Philip harrumphed, hiked up his shorts, and headed for the kitchen. "Any coffee left?"

There was no point in making a scene with him. Destiny nodded toward the pot. The phrase, *kill'em with kindness*, popped into her head. She'd learn more that way. "I'm sorry if I'm coming off too strong. I am sure you care for my mother." It was a clear lie; she didn't believe for a minute he cared about Marlene. She had to figure out what he was really up to.

Philip filled a cup and sat in the vacant chair at the small table.

Destiny blanched at the body odor that wafted toward her. She watched him slurp his coffee. "I understand you're a musician. Is that right?"

"Hm," he said with a nod. "At the JW. I play four nights a week down at Quinn's."

"Quinn's?"

"Oh, yeah. You're not from here. Quinn's is the restaurant on the beach at the JW Marriott. Tourists love that place. It's right on the sand. They have a Polynesian fire dancer that performs between my sets."

"Sounds nice. I'll get down there to see it someday." Fat chance on that.

Eleven

When Marlene got up from her nap, she seemed confused about who Philip was. She asked him twice if he was going to fix the air conditioner.

"No, Marlene," Philip said after the third time. "The A/C guy was already here. It's working fine now."

She looked at him, zero recognition crossing her face. "Then why are you here?"

Philip sighed heavily and shook his head. "Guess I'll let you ladies have some reunion time." He shot Destiny a look. "Lots of catching up to do, I imagine."

Had Marlene talked to Philip about their relationship, or more specifically, the lack thereof? It rubbed Destiny wrong that he could be passing judgement on her. She narrowed her eyes and assumed a defensive stance. "Yes, I think it would be a good idea if you left. I've got it from here."

Philip leaned to kiss Marlene, but she reared back, clearly alarmed by this motion. He reconsidered. "Okay, then. See ya soon, Marlene."

Destiny exhaled as the door closed behind him. Surely, he would be out of the picture soon enough if Marlene continued not to recognize him. He clearly didn't have the patience or the bedside manner to deal with that. Small blessings.

Marlene, on Enrique's off days, was so unpredictable. One day she would practically care for herself, choosing her own clothes and dressing herself. Other days, Destiny physically had to do everything. Recognizing Destiny was iffier. More often than not, Destiny would have to explain again who she was and that she was there to care for Marlene for a bit. Her mother's reactions varied. Even Destiny didn't know why she was there. Did that mean she was forgiving her mother?

"Come on, Mom. A little help please?" Destiny tried to lift Marlene from the bed with one arm. She wrapped Marlene's arm around her neck and lifted. But the dead weight with no help from her *patient* resulted in them ending up on the floor, tangled in arms and legs and both in tears.

"Why are you doing this to me?" wailed Marlene.

Destiny wiped away tears of frustration with her good hand. "I'm trying to help. Can you cooperate a little?"

A few minutes later, an attitude adjustment or reality check managed to remove them from the floor and be fully dressed and enjoying a breakfast of Claire Johnson's honey buns.

Within a week, Destiny had contacted an attorney who specialized in senior care recommended by Claire. It was a simple matter, and with Dr. Goldstein's affidavit, he had the paperwork filed with the county courthouse in a day. They hadn't heard another word or had a sighting of Prince Philip.

As the newly designated court-appointed guardian, Destiny paid another visit to Miss Jenson at the First American Bank of Marco. This time Miss Jenson met Destiny with an icy smile. Guess Miss Jenson had understood Destiny's parting sarcasm after all.

"Ma'am." She nodded but did not extend her hand. "I have the guardianship papers. Can we take care of my mother's accounts now?"

With the situation out of her hands, Miss Jensen made an about-face and batted her smoky-gray lined lashes. "Of course, Miss Osgood. It would be my pleasure."

Phony could have been tattooed across the woman's forehead. Talk about a complete turnaround. Now helping was a pleasure? Whatever. Was Destiny overreacting? Miss Jensen tapped long, square, purple nails on her PC and produced signature cards for Destiny to sign upon producing her I.D. Destiny handed her green military ID card. Miss Jensen frowned and asked for a driver's license.

"You do know that a military ID is valid anywhere, don't you?" When Miss Jensen didn't answer, Destiny produced her South Carolina license. *Good Lord, hadn't the woman ever dealt with military before?*

Miss Jensen gave Destiny her own debit card and an access pin to the account, as well as adding her name to the account for online use. Destiny asked for the balance and was pleased that the account wasn't completely wiped out. They concluded their business, and Destiny left, now able to access Marlene's account and set up some auto-pays for her utilities and bills.

Enrique arrived as Destiny pulled Marlene's car into the carport. Together, they walked toward the little condo. His shoulder brushed against hers as they traversed the narrow walkway. A tingling ran up her arm. She stepped into the grass to avoid touching him again. Enrique smiled and stopped, swooping his arm low to invite her to walk ahead of him on the walkway.

She stepped ahead, feeling her neck and face warm. She looked over her shoulder. "I had the pleasure of meeting Philip on Monday."

"I'm sure that was a delight. What do you think of him?"

"Not much. He claims he's taking care of her and all of us are overreacting."

Enrique stopped and touched her arm. "You know that's not true, don't you? You've seen how she goes in and out of clarity?"

Destiny gently removed his hand from her arm. "Yes, I'm aware. I wouldn't believe anything he said even if I hadn't gotten the facts straight from Dr. Goldstein. I don't know what Philip's up to, but it smells rotten to me." A memory of him sitting down at the table made her wrinkle her nose. "What if he convinced her to change her life insurance and will to leave everything to him? She isn't wealthy, but she does have assets. What else could he want?"

"I wouldn't put it past him. How would he know her financial status? The condo itself must be worth about a half a mil. Marco Island prices have skyrocketed over the years. Only so much land on an island."

Destiny gawked at him. *A half of million dollars? Wow!* "Yes, that is a possibility. I've got to keep digging. I'll figure him out and hopefully find her insurance papers and her will."

Claire Johnson was sitting with Marlene at the dining table, sharing a pot of tea. It was such a relief to have someone like Claire around, so Destiny could run errands and know Marlene was safe. And not have to depend on Enrique, or God forbid, Philip.

"Hi, look who I found in the parking lot," said Destiny.

Marlene's face gave no sign of recognition as she glanced at Enrique, then at Destiny.

Claire tapped her hand and spoke loudly. "Marlene, that's your daughter, Destiny, and your therapist, Enrique."

Marlene was senile, not deaf. "Thanks for staying with her, Claire," said Destiny. "She's very lucky to have a friend like you."

Claire lifted her stout body from the chair and carried the teapot to the counter. "It's my pleasure. Us old people have to stick together you know. We can't expect you kids to do everything. I told my son not to waste time coming to take care of me. We can take care of each other, can't we, Marlene?" She exited with a wave.

Was that a hint that she didn't want Destiny there? Or was it the rambling of an old woman? Besides, Marlene wasn't old, at least not compared to Claire, though Marlene seemed to be aging right before Destiny's eyes.

Enrique sat in the seat Claire had vacated and faced Marlene. "And how are we doing today, Miss Marlene? Are we staying out of trouble?" He gave her a wink with a big brown eye.

Marlene didn't answer him, so he pulled items from his book-bag and laid them on the table. First, he held each one up and named them: hairbrush, flashlight, coffee cup, notepad. Then he asked her to do the same.

Marlene crossed her arms and refused to speak.

Patiently, he repeated the process and asked her to name the objects.

She picked up the flashlight and whipped it across the room with a right arm any pitcher would be proud of. The flashlight banged against the wall and bounced into the wastebasket.

"Two points," Enrique praised, as if she had followed his instruction to a T. "You've got quite an arm, Miss Marlene. Ready for the World Series?"

"Get out of my house," she yelled, "or I'll throw the next thing at your head."

"Enrique's only trying to help," said Destiny.

Enrique gathered his items and shoved them back in his bag. "No, that's okay. We don't have to do this now. Shall we sit on the lanai for a while, Miss Marlene? It's a lovely day out today."

Marlene dropped the strong arm, and her shoulders visibly relaxed. "Yes, I'd like that very much." She changed moods so quickly it was hard to keep up. Together, Marlene and Enrique moved to the lanai. Destiny heard them chatting about the pelicans that made beautiful sweeping flights and clumsy awkward dives for their food. She grabbed the opportunity to log onto her laptop and search Marlene's bank account.

The good news was as Destiny had confirmed at the bank, her mother's account was not wiped out. The bad news was that someone was withdrawing $200 cash every week and had been doing so for a long time. She searched back several months, and the $200 withdrawal showed, three, four, even five months back. Some quick math showed that was $4000. Enrique had only been Marlene's therapist for six weeks. Did that rule him out as the culprit? He had said he didn't take any money, and now she could believe him. She was relieved, then wondered why she cared. She didn't even know him. Her thoughts immediately went to Philip. He certainly had the opportunity.

Destiny searched the bank's website for a place to report a fraud alert. She quickly cancelled Marlene's debit card. At least that would stop whoever was stealing from her mother. How dare someone steal from a person in this condition? There was barely enough in the account to cover a few months in the long-term care facility until somebody, most likely Angela and Sam, would have to pick up from there. Destiny certainly couldn't. She could barely afford to support herself. Finding temporary help until the facility had room for Marlene was looking less and less likely. Destiny would have to stay and take care of her as long as humanly possible.

Enrique joined Destiny on the lumpy hideaway sofa as she closed the laptop across her legs.

"She's nodded off." His eyes met hers.

Her eyes filled with unshed tears.

"It's rough sometimes, isn't it?" His voice, low and deep, soothed her jangled nerves.

Destiny nodded. "Nothing but bad news lately." She paused, unsure of how much to divulge to him. But he was clearly not the thief. "That missing debit card we were looking for? Now that I can see the account, it's clear that someone's stealing from my mother." She strummed her fingers over the top of the laptop. "How could someone do that to her, especially when she's like this? I've left a message with that A/C company that was here, but they haven't called back. Must not need business very badly if they don't even return phone calls. Or, if whoever got the message was the thief, they wouldn't call back."

"Any information on the cleaning lady? Did you find her number?"

Destiny shook her head. "Not yet. I'm putting my money on Philip. Who else could it be?"

Enrique slid his arm around the back of the loveseat, not quite touching her but clearly trying to offer comfort. That was all it took. The dam broke. She sobbed like a heartbroken teenager. What had gotten into her? She wasn't a crier. Soldiers didn't cry.

Enrique waited patiently until the wave subsided. "I'm not sure. I think the cable guy was here. But Marlene was mixed up about using the remote. And somebody brought in that new stove."

Destiny reached for a tissue from the box on the end table and glanced into the kitchen. "She's dying. Did you know that? I came here thinking I'd toss her into a home and throw away the key. But now—" she hiccupped and ducked her head.

Enrique gently pinched her chin and raised her head, so she had to look him in the eye. "Yes, I know," he whispered. "What happened between you two? Do you want to talk about it?"

Yes. No. She didn't know. She'd never talked to anyone about it except Angela. Destiny carried her burden into battle in Afghanistan, into every relationship she tried and failed, into every minute of her being. Her anger defined her, protected her. What would she have if she let that go? The words started slowly, then poured from her like lava. She couldn't seem to stop herself. The memory of that day was as alive today as it was twenty-five years earlier.

Twelve

Through Destiy's sniffles, she recounted her past to Enrique.

"I was ten years old. It was report card day.

I sat on the school bus; my book bag hugged tight to my chest. It was hard to keep from smiling, so I laughed out loud at the Baldwin brothers who were playing Monkey-in-the-Middle with geeky Lawrence Simpson's baseball cap. I knew it was bullying, but I was too happy to get all serious and righteous.

"It'd been a hard semester. Fifth-grade middle school was a lot different from grade school, and this was my third school since starting PreK. There were changing classes, lockers, study halls, but I'd worked hard with more study time every night. I did extra credit in both math and social science to make sure I aced those hard classes. I barely went outside during the week, saving my free time for Mom on Saturdays and Sundays. We shared the same kooky love of art that Dad didn't get. We either spent our time discovering new art museums or taking our pencils and chalk someplace to sketch, just the two of us. She liked landscapes; I liked drawing faces.

"I tapped the front of the book bag, imagining I could feel the heavy envelope holding my report card. Of course, I couldn't, but it was enough to know it was there. When I first saw the marks, I thought my insides would explode. It felt like jellybeans hopping around in there. I couldn't wait to get home and show my parents. They'd want to do something special to celebrate, I thought. Maybe we'd go to Dairy Queen for banana splits, and of course, they'd call Gram and Gramps to brag about me.

"Mom gave me a peck on the cheek when I entered the kitchen. Nothing was on the stove, and no smells were coming from the oven. I thought that was strange. Did she remember it was report card day? They were probably planning on taking me out to dinner to celebrate. Dinner out was even better than Dairy Queen. I gave her a quick squeeze and headed for my room. Mom wouldn't ask to see it until Dad got home. That was the ritual.

"Angela, who was five years old, was in the family room watching Bugs Bunny, her 'bankey' wrapped around the cast on her leg from when she fell off her bike two weeks before. She was home from the hospital after scaring everyone with a hemorrhage of her femoral artery and needing a blood transfusion. She waved hello, but she was so engrossed she didn't even blink away from the TV.

"In my room, I slipped the card out of the envelope and traced my fingers over the grades. I knew it was going to be the best day ever. Dad was strict about grades, but he understood how hard it was for me. He said it wasn't about what IQ you are born with; it was what you did with what you have that mattered. But I knew things came easier to him. Mom always beamed telling me about his 4.0 average all through West Point. She never went to college, only a local art school. I knew this was going to make them so proud.

"Things had been quiet between my parents lately, ever since Angela's accident on the bike. Dad acted like it was Mom's fault. She hadn't even been outside. But Dad had taken off Angela's training wheels and given her a push. We watched the front wheel swivel back and forth like a windshield wiper until she crashed right into a metal lamp post.

"Mom had a hard time adjusting to our latest move to Fort Jackson. I think South Carolina was not her favorite place in the world. My straight A's were supposed to show them what perseverance could do. They'd be as excited as me, and everything would go back to normal. I couldn't wait to see the smiles on their faces.

"Dad's car pulled in the driveway at exactly 6:20, like clockwork. Always the punctual officer, down to the nano-second. I heard hushed voices in the kitchen. I couldn't make out what they were saying. I remember thinking Mom was probably reminding him what day this was.

"When my dad called me into his den, I clasped the envelope in my hand and forced myself to walk, not run down the hall. My heart was leaping with joy, and I knew that I was grinning like the Cheshire Cat in Alice in Wonderland.

"Dad was sitting behind his desk, jacket off and sleeves rolled up to his tattooed forearms. Mom sat on the edge of the loveseat, patting her hair like she was going into an interview. Neither were smiling. Something was wrong. My heart did a little skip. I started to hand my report card to Dad, but when he began to speak, slow and deep, I pulled it back into my lap and sat next to Mom.

"Destiny," he began. "Your mother has something to tell you." He frowned at Mom, and his eyes flashed a stormy gray.

"Mom grasped my hands in hers. The envelope slipped off my lap and settled on the tan carpet at our feet. I stared at it but didn't bend to pick it up. My throat had suddenly gone dry. I wished I had popped that Double Bubble from my dresser into my mouth before I came downstairs.

'Destiny,' said Mom. "You know how much we, um …' Mom looked at Dad and then back to me, 'We … I love you, don't you?'

"All I could do was nod. Creepy-crawlies started climbing up my back.

"Mom continued. 'Sometimes people fall out of love with each other.' Her eyes settled on Dad. 'I still love your father, but I'm no longer *in* love with him.'

"I didn't understand. What the heck was that supposed to mean? What a stupid thing to say. I looked at her, then at Dad, who was examining his fingernails. I wanted to ask what all this meant, but I couldn't find any words. My heart was pounding out of my chest.

"'We're getting a divorce, honey,' Mom said, her voice shaking, making it sound staccato, like our music teacher taught us the week before. 'And I'm going away for a while.'

"My mind exploded. *Wait. What?* She was leaving? Leaving to where? Across town, another state? 'What about me?' I asked. Tears brimmed in my eyes, but I brushed them away.

"'We agreed that you should stay with your father.' Mom said. 'I'm going to be traveling, and you just started your new school. We think it's best this way.'

"Best for whom, I wanted to know. I pulled my hands from hers. I tried to grasp what she was saying, but it wasn't sinking in. Divorce? When my friend Tammy's parents got divorced, she said there was a lot of yelling and throwing things. Her mom scratched big streaks down her father's face. I saw them when he picked us up after school. Mom said it wasn't polite to bring it up, so I pretended I didn't see. My parents never fought, and I couldn't imagine anyone ever hitting Dad. Moms don't decide to walk away. Where was she going? Why didn't she want to take me?

"'What about Angela?' I croaked out between the lump in my throat.

"Mom looked down and straightened the non-existent wrinkles in her lap. 'She's too little to live with your dad,' she said. 'I'm taking her with me because she's not in school yet.'

"'Yes, she is,' I spouted. 'She's in PreK.'

"Mom shook her head. 'That doesn't count as school, honey.'"

The pressure of Enrique's arm as he put it around my shoulder brought me back to the present.

He said, "You don't have to—"

I shrugged him off. "No, let me finish. I couldn't get my head around it. Mom was leaving and taking my little sister, but she didn't want me. I thought she loved me. I thought about all the times we spent together drawing and those long talks we used to have. Didn't they mean anything to her? Angela couldn't even color in the lines.

"And Dad? He simply sat there, not saying a word. I waited for him to do something, to tell me this was a joke, crazy talk. But he didn't. He didn't say a word.

I had to get out of there. I couldn't look at either of them, but especially not her. I scooped up the envelope with the report card from the floor and tossed it at her. 'Here,' I said. 'In case you're interested. Straight A's. Happy travels.'

"The floodgates opened, and I ran for the door. In my room, I collapsed on my bed, pulling Bugsy, my favorite stuffed bunny close to my chest. I couldn't believe this was happening. What did I do to make her want to leave without me? What would we do if it was only Dad and me? He didn't know anything about taking care of kids or a house. I'd never even seen him heat soup. Mom did everything. We'd starve to death. A million scenarios ran through my head. Who was going to sketch with me? Who was going to help me with my homework when he was at work?

What if he got another unaccompanied assignment? Or deployed overseas? This couldn't be happening. Then I realized how stupid I had been. I was never special to Mom. She had only taken me to those art galleries to get out of the house and away from my father. I was nothing more than her scapegoat until she realized she could walk away. I wasn't needed anymore. So easily discarded. I wasn't nearly as cute as precious little Angela, who was a miniature Mom, tiny with curly blond hair. I reminded her of Dad, tall and skinny, frumpy brown hair that couldn't hold a curl more than ten seconds. She didn't want to look at me anymore. That was obvious if she could leave me behind. Finally, I saw it. No amount of straight A's would ever earn her love. Well, that was fine with me. I didn't need her either.

"My stomach didn't seem to agree with this logic. It felt like someone had cut a big hole right out of my middle and all my guts would pour out. Instead, I threw up the cafeteria pizza from lunch into my waste basket."

Thirteen

The weight of Max's body presses against mine. The heat from the Registan Desert is no match for the heat between us. I want to resist, to push him away, not let him get that close. But he doesn't let me, and I melt in his arms. Then in a flash, he is gone, the Humvee overturned, Max's eyes meet mine, blood dripping from his mouth, his ears, his nose, and he is gone, his body, bloody and broken on the dusty road to Kandahar.

Enrique gently tapped Destiny's shoulder. "Hey there, are you okay? You kind of left me there for a minute."

"Oh, I'm sorry. I was telling you about Marlene, right?"

"Yeah, you were. When you were a kid. Then you kind of left."

Destiny straightened up and cleared her throat. "It happens. I have flash backs sometimes."

"P.T.S.D. Pretty heavy stuff for you to deal with at ten years old. Then you were in a war and lost your arm and, I'm guessing, some guy named Max. You called out his name. It's a lot for anyone to deal with. You must have been daydreaming or having a nightmare. Your whole body was twitching."

Destiny stood. "I guess I did. Sorry. I'm not getting much sleep these days." Did he know it wasn't Marlene she was thinking about? And she sure as hell didn't want to talk to him about Max. She swept a hand through her hair. What made her think about Max? She'd been telling Enrique her story about when Marlene left. And then she was crying, and he was holding her. "I'm going to go wash my face."

Enrique nodded and flashed her that smile.

When she came back in the room, she sat at the far end of the sofa. Not far enough. She could still smell his cologne, the muskiness of his masculinity. She could still feel the heat from Max's body, too, or was that Enrique's? Yes, Max, not Enrique.

"Thank you for sharing with me. I'm sorry about what happened when you were a child," Enrique said. He scooted a little closer. "I'm not trying to say I agree with your mother, but perhaps she had a legitimate reason for leaving. Did you ever ask her?" He put an arm around her and leaned in like he was going to kiss her.

She stood to put some space between them. Who was he to think he could kiss her when she was vulnerable? Or ask her such a personal question? She didn't owe him an explanation. "Thanks for listening, but you're right. You can't possibly know. Or understand."

He raised a perfect eyebrow. "Are you sure? We all have a past."

She was suddenly angry. "Really? What's yours? Did your mother walk out on you too?" That wasn't fair. Why did she spew such nasty things from her mouth?

"No, but I watched my brother get killed right in front of me."

She froze. "Oh, my God. I'm so sorry. I'm such an idiot. Of course, you have a past. Do you want to talk about it?"

He shook his head. "Not now." He stood and moved into her personal space, his lips inches from hers.

She stepped back. "Look, Enrique. I'm not getting involved with you. Quit flirting. My only mission is to take care of Marlene. Then I'm going back to South Carolina where I belong."

"We'll see about that."

His eye had a twinkle in it. *Damn him.* She wanted to scream. Of all the arrogance. This man took the cake. Just because he was gorgeous didn't mean he could come in and sweep her off her feet. And after a bombshell like his brother being killed? Was that real? Or theatrics? Or was he looking for a sympathy fuck?

After his departure, she sat on the sofa still shaking from anger and desire. She ran her hand down her neck and across her breastbone where Enrique—no, Max, had been kissing her. Impossible. It was only a dream.

She tried to brush the thoughts out of her mind. She sat down with Marlene's checkbook and logged on the bank website to look at Marlene's account again. Marlene had done well for herself. A sense of pride swelled in Destiny's chest. Good for her. Did that mean there was hope for her, too, as an artist? Had she inherited her mother's talent? Destiny paid the overdue bills and set up auto-pays for the future.

But Marlene was far from wealthy, and at the high cost of long-term care, it would only last a few months. Two more $200.00 cash withdrawals in the last week. She'd been with Marlene the whole time. There was no way she was withdrawing the cash. They were ATM withdrawals. Somebody had her debit card and her passcode. Thank God the card was void now. But who had been doing this? She ticked the possibilities off on her fingers: the internet guy, the stove guy, the housekeeper, Enrique, Philip. It would be easy for anyone to pick up her card if she'd left it out in the open. Wouldn't she have pulled it out to pay them if they accepted payments on a Square reader or something like that? She could have set it on the table, and they could have picked it up easily. But then how did they get her password? Didn't sound likely. Destiny looked at the stack of bills and miscellaneous receipts. Could a stranger have hacked Marlene's card somehow if she'd left it somewhere? The location codes on the ATMs indicated two different addresses. They were only six days apart, the last being only the day before Destiny had cancelled the card. Surely the bank could determine the exact locations of the ATMs and pull the security camera tapes. She had to get back to the bank.

Destiny tiptoed to the door to her mother's room. Not a sound. That was good, for several reasons. She thought back to the moments with Enrique when he had almost kissed her. What was happening here? It didn't make sense he'd be attracted to her. Angela, sure. Small, blond, stacked Angela. But Destiny? She caught a look in the mirror of her muscular, but flat body, her mousy mess of a hair. And her arm. Imagine taking off your clothes to see that. Which was worse? The robot-hand or the ugly stump? Who wouldn't be repulsed by that? Her mind was a jumble between Enrique's touch and Max's memory. Max, when she was whole. And he was alive. She shook her head hard. *Stop it. It's only memories.* Enrique is not Max. They couldn't be more different.

She paced back and forth in the small living/dining room. She needed to clear her head and take care of business. If Claire could come over and sit with her mother, she'd go back to the bank. Who knew how long it would take to track all this down, but it had to be done.

"Claire," Destiny said into the phone. "I need to run a few errands. Would you mind sitting with Marlene? I shouldn't be too long."

"No problem. I'll be right there. I was going to put a pie into the oven, but I'll wait until you get back. Give me a few minutes."

Thank God for people like Claire Johnson.

Fourteen

Natalie Jensen was on vacation when Destiny arrived at the bank, but the presiding manager, a man closer to her age, Noah Smithfield, was pleasant and eager to help. With very few clicks, he identified the locations of the last two ATM withdrawals. One was at the Walgreens on Tamiami Trail in Naples, and the last one was from the Publix grocery store on South Barfield on Marco Island. He contacted the managers of each. He hung up the phone with a frown. "Unfortunately, the camera was broken at the Walgreens location in Naples."

She let out a sigh in exasperation. *Great.* "And the other location … at the grocery store?"

"Publix sends all their camera tapes to the corporate office at the end of each day. They will have to contact the corporate office in Lakeland. It'll take a few days."

"I already cancelled her card, but I still want to know who was doing this."

"I understand. Should I issue a new card for your mother? We're very sorry for this, and we'll reinstate the funds from those last two transactions to her account as soon as the fraud department can verify that she wasn't making the withdrawals. If we determine that any other withdrawals were fraudulent, we'll take care of those as well."

"I don't know if my mother will ever be able to complete banking transactions on her own again, so if I have a card, I think that's sufficient. According to her bank statements, it looks like twenty or more withdrawals over the last several months." She stood to leave. "Thank you so much for your help. You'll contact me as soon as you find out about the grocery store transaction?"

"Yes, of course. We'll get to the bottom of it, Captain Osgood. And thank you for your service."

She should have corrected him, but it felt good to be recognized for her service. How did he know? Had the haughty Miss Jenson mentioned it? "Thank you, sir."

Back in the car, Destiny breathed a sigh of relief. Since she stopped the fraud, did she care who was responsible? Did she want a confrontation? Yes, she did. Whoever was doing this should be punished. Arrested, even sent to jail. Who would steal from a woman with dementia?

Claire was dozing on the sofa when Destiny stepped through the door. Old people sure slept a lot. Destiny touched her shoulder gently. "Claire, I'm back. You can go bake your pie now."

Claire blinked a few times and stretched. She stood slowly and pulled herself up by leaning on the end table for support. "Oh, hello, Destiny. Your mother hasn't made a sound. I didn't want to disturb her, so I sat here and waited. I guess I dozed off."

"It's fine, Claire. Again, thanks. I'll peek in on her now. She's been asleep a long time."

The door to Marlene's room was still closed, but Destiny turned the knob and opened it slowly. "Marlene, Mom, are you okay? You've been sleeping—" She stopped mid-sentence.

Marlene was not in her bed.

Destiny looked around the small room, checked either side of the bed in case she had fallen. Not there. "Mom?" Destiny opened the adjoining bathroom door. Nobody. Panic seized her chest. Where was Marlene? Destiny twirled around the bedroom, hoping she'd find her sitting in her chair or standing in the doorway. But she was gone.

"Claire!" Destiny hollered. "Are you still here? My mother is gone."

Claire appeared in the doorway. "What do you mean, gone? You said she was sleeping. I never even opened the door."

"You didn't check on her?" The truth was, Destiny hadn't checked on her either, not since she'd heard her snoring before she left for the bank. How long had she been gone? Where would she have gone?

"The slider." Claire pointed. The sliding glass door from Marlene's bedroom to the lanai was open about an inch.

This wasn't good. Was she in today's world or in some dimension from her past? Destiny picked up the phone and called 9-1-1.

Fifteen

Marlene

Oh my. The clock beside my bed reads 2:45. Why am I still not dressed? I'm going to be late picking Destiny up from school. I throw on the first clothes I see, grey capris and a soft cotton tunic. Funny, I don't remember these clothes. Not my style at all, more for old people. I run a hand over my soft, round belly. I must have bought them for the pregnancy. Elastic and roomy.

No time to waste worrying about clothes, I have to get to Destiny. I slip out the sliding glass door and hurry down the sidewalk. It isn't until I step on a pebble that I realize my feet are bare. Oh well, it is warm out, unusually so for fall. I breathe in the fresh air. Soon the chill of winter would be on us. I'd enjoy this gift from God.

At the corner, everything looks unfamiliar. A queasiness rumbles in my stomach. Which way should I go? One way I see shops and apartment buildings. The other is houses. The school must be near the houses, right? I pull the tunic tighter around me. Why don't I recognize any of this? I search my brain. Had we moved again, and I'd forgotten? Oh, the woes of a military wife, new cities every few years. That must be it. *Don't panic, Marlene.* This is silly. Of course, the school would be right down this way.

But it isn't. I turn down the next street and pick up my pace. Oh, dear, Destiny will be waiting for me in a new school. She'll be scared. My heart beats loudly in my ears.

"Ouch." I stub my toe on a raised crack in the sidewalk. I go down hard on both knees. My toe is bleeding, and both knees are scraped. And I'm clearly lost. Tears fill my eyes. "Damn you, Frank. Damn the Army." Why couldn't we stay in one place with one house like everyone else? Now I've resorted to swearing. What next? Should I take up smoking?

I pull myself to my feet and brush off the pebbles from my knees. There's nothing I can do about my toe. I turn left and head down the next street. Hold on, Dezi. I'm coming. If I can only find you. I need to focus. My throat feels like sandpaper. Why isn't there a policeman anywhere when you need one? He could point me to the school.

Three or four blocks later, I wind up at a dead end with a wide body of water in front of me. A river? A lake? Where am I? A wooden bench beckons me to sit. My toe has stopped bleeding, but my whole body hurts from the pain in my toe to my bruised knees to my aching heart. I am lost. A panic attack seizes my chest and crushes it until I can't breathe. My head is a blur of things that don't make sense; Frank screaming at me and calling me a whore. A man. A different man with his arms around me, kissing me. Dezi, but not my Dezi, older, telling me to leave her alone.

I bury my face in my hands. Please make this stop. What is happening to me? Somebody help me.

A man with a long ponytail rushes across the grass and toward me. "Marlene, what are you doing here? Are you all right?"

I don't know this man. How does he know my name? Do I dare tell a stranger that I'm lost? Frank will have a fit, embarrassing him like that.

"No, no, I'm all right," I say without conviction.

He looks at my bare foot, the one with the bloodied toe.

I try to pull my capris over my scuffed knees.

"Marlene, it's me. Philip." He reaches for me, like he's going to take my arm.

I scoot away from him so he can't grab me. "Can you point me in the direction of the elementary school? I'm late picking up my daughter."

His eyebrows shoot up. "Marlene, your children are grown. And you're injured. Let me take you home. Destiny is worried about you."

How does he know my daughter, Destiny? Is he a child predator? If he has her held hostage somewhere, I'd follow him to the ends of the earth to get to her. "Do you know where she is? She should be at school, waiting for me."

The man harrumphs as if he's irritated with me. "She's at home. Now, come on, Marlene. Let me take you home." He points to a beat-up old car.

I may be confused, but I'm not stupid enough to get into a car with a stranger.

"No. I don't know you, and I'm not getting in any car with you."

"Marlene. Be reasonable. It's time to go home."

I huff and cross my arms over my chest. "If you plan on accosting me, you have another thing coming. I'll scream. Call the police. You get away from me." The very idea. I can see it in the papers now. A woman gets abducted by a strange man on her way to pick up her daughter at school. Well, not this woman. I press my hands into my lap and look down. My gosh. My knees are all skinned up, and I have a bloody toe. "Did you do this to me? Help!" I shout. "Help, this man's trying to hurt me."

The man raises his hands. "Marlene, I didn't touch you. Have it your way—I'm outta here." He waves his arms heads back to his car.

I breathe a little easier once he is gone. This never would have happened if we'd stayed in one place. It's all Frank's fault. I touch my hand to my stomach. New cities, new schools, new friends. And I'll have to go through all this again when this little one is born. It's too much. I'm not cut out to be an Army wife. I should tell him tonight to make a choice—me or the Army. Of course, that's a silly ultimatum. He couldn't give up his career, and I'd never say a word to him. I never speak up to Frank. I'm the good Army wife, whether I always like it or not. Still, it felt good to think about it, even if only for a minute. Wait, what am I doing worrying about what to say to Frank when I still need to find Destiny? Now, how do I get to the school?

Sixteen

Destiny identified herself as Captain Osgood without thinking and explained everything to the police dispatcher who seemed to be taking an excruciating long time getting it all down. Address, her name, Marlene's name, her age, her medications. Destiny scurried for one of the bills in her purse to confirm the right address.

What was Marlene wearing? Destiny had no idea. Her nightgown sat on the edge of the bed. She must have changed into something.

The dispatcher promised to send an officer right out. "Stay put."

Destiny needed to be out looking for her mother, not sitting there waiting for the police officer. She hung up and walked to the end of the parking lot. Looking both ways, she hoped she'd see her mother sitting on a bench or talking to a neighbor. Nothing.

Claire joined Destiny on the sidewalk. "Any sign of her?"

If there was, would Destiny be standing there looking into nothingness? She shook her head. Beads of sweat broke out on her forehead and dripped off her nose. Was it panic or the damn Florida humidity?

"Does she have any friends around here where she might have gone?"

"I don't know. Did you try Philip? Or someone from the Art Center? She used to be involved with them when she was more lucid."

"Philip. Yes. I've got his number on the white board. And the Art Center? Okay. Good. Is that walking distance?"

"Oh, heavens. no. It's at the south end of the island."

Destiny ran back into the condo to get Philip's number. She tried the number on the white board. 239-555-2773. Wrong number. Damn his scribble. Was that an 8, or a 3? She dialed 239-555-2778.

A voice recording said the mailbox was full and could not accept any more messages. Great. She slammed the phone down on the receiver. The voice message didn't identify the owner, so she still wasn't sure she'd dialed the right number.

Two police cars pulled into the parking lot. They hadn't had the sirens on, but the red and blue swirling lights flashed a bizarre haze on the trees and pavement.

A young officer with a short handlebar mustache extended a hand toward her. "Captain Osgood? I'm Lieutenant Pavlovic." He nodded toward a younger, female officer speaking into the radio attached to her shoulder. "This is Officer Gaines."

"Yes, sir. And actually, it's Miss Osgood now. Or Destiny. Still acclimating to civilian life. Thank you for coming so quickly. I went to the bank, and when I came back, she was gone."

He nodded. "Army? Thank you for your service." He wrote something in his little black notebook. "Your mother, correct? Is she incapable of being left alone?"

"She wasn't alone." Destiny gestured in Claire's direction. "Her neighbor, Claire Johnson, came and sat with her. She, Mom, that is, has Alzheimer's. She goes in and out of clarity, so we never leave her alone."

"Well, then, how did she disappear?"

Claire came up beside Destiny and hooked an arm through hers. "It's all my fault. Destiny asked me to stay with Marlene, but she was asleep, so I didn't disturb her. Her bedroom door was closed. I should have checked on her." Claire pulled a handkerchief from her housecoat pocket and dabbed at her eyes.

"I didn't tell her to look. It's not her fault," Destiny said. The poor woman was distraught enough. She didn't need anyone blaming her.

Lieutenant Pavlovic gestured toward the front door. "May we go inside?"

The four of them walked the few steps back to the condo. Destiny sent an urgent text to Enrique.

> **Marlene is missing. Wandered off. Need help NOW.**

The officers went into the bedroom, wrote more notes on their little pads, and snapped a picture of the open sliding glass door.

"Do you have a recent picture of her?" Lieutenant Pavlovic asked. "What about friends she could have gone to visit?"

Embarrassed that she didn't carry a picture of her own mother in her wallet, Destiny scoured through drawers trying to find something. Nothing.

Claire pulled a photo album down from the bookcase in the corner. "Maybe there's something in here."

A text came through from Enrique.

I'm on it. Did you call the police?

Destiny sat on the edge of the armchair, sent YES to Enrique, and scanned through the photo album. Her mouth gaped open at what she found. Dozens of clippings of her, her graduation from West Point with her father, the Honorable Discharge ceremony, a picture of her in Afghanistan in full combat gear Was that Max in the background? She felt a familiar tug at her heart. Where did Marlene get these? Had she been following Destiny's every move her whole life? There were pictures of Angela's children and Angela's family on vacation in Disney Land. But no photos of Marlene.

"Surely there's a picture of her taken at my sister's wedding, but it'd be four years old now." Destiny said. "Shouldn't we be out looking for her instead of sitting here going through picture albums? She could be hurt, or lost, or anything."

"We already have cars driving the neighborhood. The officers will question any woman walking alone, but it'd help to have a photo. At least give us a description."

Destiny ran a hand through her short, dark hair. "A description. Let's see. Fifty-five-years-old but looks closer to late sixties. Short, bottle-blond hair, about five feet four inches, about one hundred forty pounds."

"Fifty-five? That's young for dementia. Are you sure she didn't go visit some friends or go shopping?"

Destiny shook her head. "She has early onset Alzheimer's."

Officer Gaines smile vanished. "I see. Unfortunately, you described ninety-five percent of the female population here on the island. We'll need a little more than that to go by."

"Wait," Claire said. "I think I have a group photo from a condo party we had a few months ago. Let me run home and get it."

"That would be most helpful, Mrs. Johnson," said Officer Gaines.

Lieutenant Pavlovic turned to Destiny. "We issued a Silver Alert. But we don't have much to go on."

"Silver Alert?"

"Yes, here in south Florida, we lose more elderly people than we do children. Think Amber Alert for seniors. Most are found within an hour or so. They've usually wandered off without telling anyone. It's rare that any harm comes to them. I'm sure your mother is fine."

Destiny knew he was trying to be reassuring, but his words fell empty on her ears. Marlene—her responsibility—was sick, and now she was gone. Running a sweaty hand down her pant leg, she gulped, trying to find some saliva in her dry throat. "I need a glass of water. Would you care for some?" She rose to head into the tiny kitchen.

The female officer pressed a hand to her shoulder, lowering Destiny to the sofa. "Let me get that for you, Captain, Sorry, *Miss* Osgood. You're understandably upset."

Destiny nodded in appreciation. *Oh God. Angela.* "I should call my sister. She may have an idea where our mother went. She was caring for her before I got here." She reached for her cell phone.

Angela picked up on the first ring. "Dezi, everything okay?"

Destiny sipped at the water. "No, it's not. Our mother is missing. Do you have any idea where she might have gone?"

"Missing? What do you mean missing? How long has she been gone?"

Destiny filled her in on everything that had happened.

"How long, Destiny?"

She honestly didn't know. "I'd been gone about forty-five minutes at the bank. But she could have left before that when I was talking to Enrique. It could be more than an hour." She felt like shit. She couldn't even look after one little old lady. What was wrong with her?

Claire came running back through the door with a snapshot. They crowded together to take a look. The officers were right. Every one of the females in the photo had the same shade of hair, most styled almost identically, and quite close in height and weight, the only difference being that Marlene looked slightly younger.

Destiny pointed out her mother, seated to the far left a broad smile on her face.

"May we have this?" Officer Pavlovic asked.

Claire hesitated for a second. "It's my only copy, but of course. I'm sure I can get another from one of the members."

"We will return it once we find her," said Officer Gaines. A buzz came through the walkie-talkie on her shoulder. "We've located a woman on a bench down by the water on Edington Street. She seems a bit confused. She's with a man. He says his name is Enrique Lopez, her home health aide."

Pavlovic's eyebrows shot up. "Lopez." He turned to Destiny "Does she know him?"

"Affirmative," said the officer. "She says she is Mrs. Frank Osgood."

Enrique found her. Destiny breathed a sigh of relief. "That's her."

"That's the one. If she's amenable, bring her back here to the Marco Vista Condos on Bald Eagle Drive. Unit 103A."

"Ten-four."

Pavlovic smiled. "See, I told you. Most of the time everything works out fine. You did the right thing calling us, though. We are always here to help. We'll stick around until she's home safe and sound, then we'll be on our way."

"Thank you, Lieutenant." Destiny tried to offer a smile back but knew it looked forced.

Marlene's home phone rang, and Destiny answered.

"This is Philip. Thought you should know, I found Marlene sitting on a bench on Edington Street. She didn't know me. I tried to get her to go with me, but she wouldn't budge. Started screaming about me assaulting her. Get the police to pick her up. You need to keep her on a leash."

Destiny's shoulders tensed. "I'll keep that in mind, Philip. Enrique's got her. Emergency abated."

"That woman's bat-shit crazy. I'm done."

"Well, so glad you are concerned." Destiny hoped he caught the sarcasm and hung up. Although she was grateful the situation was now under control, she had to face the fact that Marlene couldn't be trusted alone for even a second unless she was someplace safer, like a home. What if she had gotten hurt or wandered even farther? Or, God forbid, what if Angela had not hidden the car keys? She could have taken the car and driven off somewhere. This was much more serious than forgetting her name, not being able to name a hairbrush or not recognizing her daughter. Her safety was at stake here. Destiny had been foolish to think this was going to be an easy fix: get her some therapy and find a nice little home to put her in, tucked away out of sight, out of mind.

An uncomfortable but familiar knot settled in her stomach. *Wasn't that exactly what Mom did when she walked out on me? And I was only a child. Did she ever think about what that felt like to me, alone and afraid and feeling unloved? How could she do that?* Destiny shook her head to come back to the present. A military psychiatrist had explained that these feelings were all part of childhood PTSD she had never dealt with. Some days were easier than others to shake them off.

The real question was, could Destiny do that to Marlene? Destiny glanced at the photo album sitting on the coffee table. Had her mother been trying to make up for leaving by tracing her daughter's every move, by sticking pictures in an album? Was that supposed to make it all okay? Marlene didn't know anything about the real Destiny Osgood. How could she? She was never there. Of course, that wasn't 100% true. Angela wouldn't have let her forget. She would have hounded Marlene about her. Destiny wondered if this album was actually Angela's doing. It would make more sense. Angela never stopped loving her.

Angela. Crap. She'd forgotten she was still hanging on the line.

"Hello? Hello? Destiny? Are you still there?"

"Yeah, Ange. I'm here. Enrique found her. She's safe. Sorry to alarm you. I'll give you a call back when she's home and everything settles down."

"Um, okay." Angela didn't sound very reassured, but she hung up, leaving Destiny holding the phone until it started buzzing.

Seventeen

The cruiser pulled into the yard, lights flashing. Thank God, they didn't have the siren on. Enrique's car pulled in beside it, Marlene next to him in the passenger seat. She refused a hand when an officer tried to help her out of the car. She was in a mood. Did she know she'd been lost, causing them all kinds of anxiety?

Marlene came through the front door in a huff, feet stomping, arms crossed across her chest. "What's wrong with you, Destiny? You called the police on me? Whatever for?"

"Mom." Destiny kept her voice soft and non-combative. "I came home from the bank and couldn't find you. Claire didn't know where you were either. We were worried about you."

"Can't a woman go for a walk in her own neighborhood without it being a capital offense? Go back to wherever you came from. I don't need a babysitter." She turned to Enrique. "And same goes for you."

She did need a babysitter, but she didn't need Destiny. Marlene hadn't needed her daughter for a very long time. When would that stop hurting? Marlene would be better off, happier if Destiny wasn't around. Enrique and Claire could handle her. And Destiny could go back to her neat little life in South Carolina. *Oh, stop. This isn't about you. It's about what's best for Marlene.*

The truth was that Destiny needed Marlene. She needed to keep her at home and keep her memory as clear as possible if she ever wanted answers. Did that mean she did want answers now? She deserved them, but when did she begin to care? She could put her life in South Carolina on hold, at least until she knew the truth about why Marlene left. Then, she could settle her in a home where she would be safe. And not Destiny's responsibility.

Destiny squared her shoulders. "I'm sorry, Mmm … Mom. I really am." She turned to the officers with a sheepish smile. "False alarm. Thanks for everything. I think you can go now."

Lieutenant Pavlovic wrote something in his little notebook and tipped his hat. Such a gentleman. "Glad it all turned out okay. Have a nice day." He handed the photograph back to Claire. "Thank you." And he was gone, along with Officer Gaines and their police cars with flashing lights.

Several white-haired neighbors clustered in the neighboring yard, housecoats and tongues a wagging. Claire would have to deal with them.

"Okay, all's well that ends well." Did she actually say that? She shrugged sheepishly at Enrique and mouthed a silent thank you. She turned to her mother. "How about a nice glass of iced tea and some Lorna Doones? I know they're your favorite."

Marlene huffed a little more but moved into the kitchen, grabbed the cookie tin, and slammed it a little too hard on the dining table. Destiny guessed that meant she would like tea and cookies.

Destiny boiled the water and poured it into one of the many china teapots scattered across Marlene's counters and shelves. A faint memory of her grandmother's teapots and cups made her smile.

"Is this one of Grandma's pots? I remember some of them. They were so pretty, and she was always afraid I'd break them, but she still let me pour from them when I was not much older than Angela's daughter is now."

A smile spread across Marlene's face, her features visibly softening. "Yes, this one sat on her credenza. She always said to use the good things, not to waste them sitting around on shelves getting dusty. I try to use a different one every day. You made a good choice. I haven't used this one for at least a month."

Destiny let the tea steep, then poured the tea into a delicate cup with black roses on the sides and around the rim of the saucer and placed it in front of Marlene. No mugs for her. Always a cup and saucer. It was a little like playing dress-up when she was a child. It felt good. She sipped at her tea in a cup decorated with yellow daisies. Apparently, any hard feelings were forgotten.

"Mom, would you like it if I moved to Florida to be here with you full time?"

Marlene turned toward her. The blankness in her eyes said it all. "Excuse me, do I know you?"

Eighteen

Destiny was more than happy to see Enrique show up for his appointment with Mom two days after the big scare. He had silently slipped out while they were drinking their tea. Was it relief in his expertise with Marlene or something about the way he looked in those tight jeans and black T-shirt pulled tight across his chest?

"How's my favorite girl today?" he asked.

"Fine," Marlene and Destiny answered in unison.

Destiny's ears burned. *Damn this fair skin.*

He winked. Was a blush deepening his copper skin? "Good to hear. What's new these days? Any unscheduled trips?"

Destiny gulped. Was she feeling sparks? Oh, not good. Definitely bad. She needed to clean up things there and get out before things got out of hand. They both looked to Marlene to see if she remembered the scare from two days ago.

Marlene didn't answer.

"Claire Johnson practically tackled me trying to get to me first. Thought I was some kind of hero," said Enrique. "Hardly. I found Marlene sitting on a bench on Eddington Street. Thankfully she knew who I was and didn't scream. But she wasn't happy about the police cars and lights flashing. I bet the neighbors were having a time."

"A few huddled next door talking," said Destiny. "But the important thing is Marlene is fine. She simply went on a little walk, isn't that right, Mom?" The word *Mom* still stuck in her throat, but Destiny was making an effort.

Marlene looked up with one raised eyebrow. "What are you talking about? I haven't left this building in three months."

Destiny matched her raised eyebrow and gave her head a miniscule shake.

Enrique nodded. "Well, why don't we work on some of those memory skills today. We'll play a little game. I'll ask you a question, and you answer. Okay?"

Marlene harrumphed but gave a slight nod.

"What year were you born?"

"1966."

"What city were you born in?"

"Columbus, Ohio, of course."

"Great. How many children do you have?"

"Two—two girls."

"Where do they live?"

"Angela lives with me. Destiny lives with her father in South Carolina."

Enrique gave a slight nod but kept his expression neutral. "Okay, how old are your girls?"

"Angela is eight; Destiny is thirteen, no, fourteen last month."

"Do you know what year it is?"

Marlene looked up, a confused look on her face. "Um, 1990? No, that can't be right. If Angela is eight, it must be 1994. Is that right?"

Destiny shifted uncomfortably against the kitchen counter. Why was he trying to force this on her? Enrique knew what stage Marlene was in. What was this accomplishing besides irritating her? And why did Marlene choose 1994 to be in? Not a good year for her.

Before Destiny could speak, Enrique pulled a calendar from his backpack. "You've lost a few years, Marlene. What does it say on this calendar?"

A sun-spotted hand flew to Marlene's mouth. "2020?" She looked astonished. "Is that right?"

"Marlene, I want you to look at that woman standing by the sink." He gestured toward Destiny. "Do you know who that is?"

Destiny froze. A breeze from the open window blew a stray lock of hair into her face. She wanted to brush it away, pretend it was all casual, all cool. What did it matter if Marlene knew who she was? It wasn't Marlene's fault. Destiny knew that, in her head. But it *did* matter. Her heart shredded into tiny pieces on the days her mother didn't recognize her. She felt abandoned all over again. Why? She'd given up on her mother years ago. Then why did her self-worth take a nosedive every time Marlene didn't recognize her?

For what felt like an eternity, Marlene examined her. She stared at Destiny's hair, that unmanageable lock that swept across her face. Their eyes met, but she was looking at her eyes — the color or shape — not at Destiny as a person. Then her gaze trailed down her body.

Destiny's heart sank. She didn't know her.

Suddenly, Marlene's head bounced up, the light dawning in her eyes. "Destiny," she said triumphantly. "That's my daughter, Destiny. She's a soldier, you know." Pride puffed out her chest, and she sat up taller.

Destiny wanted to rush toward her and hug her. *She knows me. She knows me.* "Right, Mom. It's me. I'm here to stay with you awhile."

She'd stay as long as Marlene let her, especially when she looked with love in her eyes like she was doing now. She could forgive her anything — if she kept looking at Destiny like that. Destiny couldn't hold back. She dropped to her knees in front of Marlene and wrapped her arms around her waist, her head resting in her lap.

Marlene stroked her hair, "There, there, sweetie. It's okay. Mommy is here."

The feel of Marlene's hand, soft and warm across Destiny's forehead, stroking, stroking, stroking, sent her mind back to another time.

I'm eight-years-old. Mom and I are walking hand-in hand, carrying our sketch pads to the park in Fort Belvoir where Dad is stationed. It's fall in Virginia, and with every gust of cool air that stirs the branches above us, the leaves float to the ground like a crimson, orange, and yellow waterfall.

We're practicing with colored pencils. Mom captures the landscape colors perfectly on her pad. I'm drawing a child playing in the sand box. The colors are all wrong. His face too red, his arms too short and pale. A gangly boy, all long, stick-arms and legs, chases a football that rolls into our little space on the grass. He looks over my shoulder and snorts. "Ha, that looks like an Injun." He cups a hand over his mouth. "Woo, woo, woo. Woo, woo woo." My heart sinks. Tears well up, and I throw myself into Mom's lap, hiding the shame of my terrible work.

The boy runs off, tossing his football in a long pass across the lawn.

"Don't you pay any attention to him," Mom coos into my ear. Her hand caresses my hair softly, brushing it off my forehead. "I bet he can't draw a lick. Probably draws stick people like a three-year-old."

I giggle at the thought but keep my head in her warm lap. I could lie there all day letting her stroke my hair.

Destiny opened her eyes. She wasn't eight years old, and the moment was gone. Lifting her head, she looked up at Marlene. "Mom?"

Nineteen

Marlene

A young woman is kneeling on the floor in front of me, her arms wrapped around my waist, her head in my lap. She has an artificial arm. I touch her hair, run my fingers through her silky chocolate strands. It's comforting somehow, but I have no idea who she is.

She must know me, or why would she be here with her arms wrapped around me in an embrace? This is close, intimate even. Her body molds into mine like it belongs here.

I continue to run fingers softly over her forehead. She nestles in deeper, somehow finding comfort in my touch. It's not an unpleasant feeling, and I lean my head back so I can see her face more clearly. I can make out the fresh face of a woman in her mid-thirties. Straight nose, nice features, lovely even if I can't say beautiful. Except for her eyelashes—thick and dark, curled up naturally against her closed lids. Not mascara—natural.

The arm puzzles me, but I don't want to embarrass her by bringing it up. Whatever happened to this poor girl? I want to speak—to ask who she is, but it feels wrong, and I hate to break this serene moment. My hand pauses on her wide forehead. I brush her hair away. She has a widow's peak. A stab of memory. Someone close to me had that same hairline. I saw myself pulling a brush through dark straight hair, away from a small forehead with its widow's peak, affixing it in a high ponytail at the back of her head.

Who? When? The memory is gone. I look around the room with the woman in my lap. Not only do I not know this girl, this woman, I don't know this room. Where am I? I'm sitting in a small, tufted chair beside sliding glass doors looking out to trees and water beyond a stretch of grass. Palm trees? Water? None of this makes any sense. The fronds from the palms wave to me on the other side of the glass like they know me.

This isn't right. How did I get here? My heart pounds loudly in my ears. I pull my hands away and raise them in defense. I want to scream, terror ripping the words from my mouth.

The young woman releases her arms from my waist and looks up. "Mom?"

"Who are you?"

"It's me, Destiny."

No. That can't be. Destiny's a child. Yes, the child with the dark hair and widow's peak. I look closely into the woman's eyes. It can't be.

The one that calls herself by my daughter's name rocks back on her heels and stands. She's tall, almost muscular on a thin frame. Her eyes show so much pain. "You knew who I was a moment ago. Didn't she, Enrique?"

A copper-toned man standing off in the corner nods. I hadn't noticed him before. A strange man in a strange place. I pull myself in, clutching an ugly green sweater around me tighter. "Who?"

He smiles. A wide broad smile shows gleaming white teeth. "It's okay, Marlene. I'm Enrique, your home health aide, and this is Destiny, your daughter. You're safe in your own little condo here on Marco Island in Florida. You're fine. Nobody's going to hurt you."

His words are buttery smooth and calming, but they make no sense.

"Frank?" I finally blurt out. "Where's my husband?"

The man and woman exchange a look, like they know something I don't.

"Tell me." My voice gets stronger as my fear turns into rage. "What have you done with Frank and my children? Where are my children, Destiny and Angela?"

The man steps toward me.

I shriek. "Don't touch me."

He raises his hands in resignation. "Okay, okay. No one's going to touch you. How about we sit quietly here for a little while we all catch our breath." He sits down on the foot of the bed as far away from me as he can. The young woman, arms crossed, leans against a white provincial dresser.

Good. At least he isn't going to grab me. At least not yet. If they make one move toward me, I'll scream at the top of my lungs. Surely someone will hear me. I scan the room with my eyes. There's a phone on the bedside table. If I try to grab it to call someone, would they stop me before I got to it? Probably. I'll sit here for a bit. See what they do. Frank will show up.

Twenty

Destiny and Enrique sat at the small dining table, coffee getting cold in front of them. She slumped lower in the chair and tucked a strand of hair behind her ear. "She's getting worse, isn't she?"

Enrique glanced at the closed bedroom door and nodded. "I'm sorry. I thought it would take longer. She's not improving, as we expected, but the rules for Medicaid are different."

"Why do you torment her with trying to remember things when she clearly cannot. It seems cruel."

"I'm not trying to be cruel. I *am* trying to trigger current memories, not only those in the distant past. The longer we can keep her present, the better off she'll be. But any continued therapy is contingent on it working, showing progression or at least stability, or Medicaid will stop paying."

Destiny looked up, her eyes slowly registering what that meant. "You'll stop coming? No, Enrique. You can't let that happen. Marlene needs you." Her voice dropped to a whisper. "I need you."

He reached across the table and pressed her hand into his. "Why, Destiny? Why do you need me?" His eyes bore a hole deep in her soul. "Only to care for Miss Marlene? Tell me there is more. Tell me you want me for me, not the therapy."

Destiny pulled her hand away slowly. Why had she said she needed him? She was opening a place in her heart that she'd kept locked tight. She couldn't let him in. It would be the same story, all over again. Everybody leaves. And she'd be left shattered and alone again. "I … I can't." She wrapped her good hand around the sleeve covering her prosthetic.

His face clouded over, and he stood, turning his back and leaning on the counter. For several minutes, neither spoke.

Destiny could hear her heart pounding in her ears. *Let him in. Don't lose him.*

Enrique's voice came out low and pained. "What happened to make you close down like this? There must be more than your parents splitting up. Talk to me, Destiny."

A prickling started at the back of her neck, and her gut twisted in knots. She bit her lip to keep her thoughts from spilling out. How dare he? Her parents hadn't simply split up. Her mother abandoned her. She may have been the first to leave, but Enrique, sure as hell, wasn't going to be the last. Why didn't he get that? Finally, she spat words at him. "I'm sorry my life feels trivial to you. I'm sorry my past interferes with your fantasy plans for us. There is no us. There never was. There never *will* be. I'm damaged goods, okay?"

Enrique stood there, his back still to her. Under his T-shirt, the muscles in his back rippled at her words.

Slowly he turned and faced her. His voice was low, calm, and patient. "Your life is not trivial. I didn't mean to imply it was. I'm sorry. I know you have feelings for me. I feel it. It's not a fantasy. I'm falling in love with you, Destiny. Let me in. Let me help you." A small smile crept across his face. "You may be a little damaged, but so am I. You are not irreparable. And I'm good at fixing things."

To Destiny's horror, tears rimmed her eyes. Soldiers weren't supposed to cry. Even if she was a civilian now, after all. What was wrong with her? This was not the way it was supposed to go. He should yell back, storm out, say he never wanted to see her again. Not be understanding. Not be wonderful.

He stepped forward and wrapped her in his arms. She struggled for a second, but he tightened his hold, and she gave in to his warmth, his love.

"What things are broken about you? You're perfect," she said into his shoulder.

He pulled back enough to look her in the face. A sad twist to his lips, not a smile, not a frown. He reached over and lifted the legs of his jeans.

Destiny jumped back, aghast. Both of his legs were badly scarred. They were thin and pale. They didn't match the rest of his copper-toned, well-defined body. "What happened? Tell me."

He lifted her chin to face him. "Okay, I will." But instead of talking, he slowly kissed away the wet on her eyelids. Then he kissed her nose, her chin. His mouth met hers and everything got hazy.

She kissed him back, at first hesitantly, but he sucked her tongue into his mouth and pressed his body more tightly against her. An urgency, a hunger coursed through her veins. She wanted him. She shouldn't. She forced herself to pull away.

"Ah, Destiny. Why do you do that? Always pull away from me." Without making eye contact, he grabbed his satchel from the back of the chair. "I give up. Let me know if you change your mind. I've gotta go."

She reached out to touch his arm. "Don't." Enrique was right; as bad as Marlene's abandonment was, it wasn't all of it.

"Okay, I'll tell you." she relented. "Don't leave. But only if you'll tell me what happened to you. Enrique, you're right. I am attracted to you. But I don't even know you. We can't do this"—she motioned between them—"at least not yet."

Enrique hesitated, then took a seat on the small sofa in the living room.

Destiny checked on Marlene, who was sound asleep, then joined him. Destiny began. "Everything in my life prior to my mother leaving seemed perfect. I thought there was something special between us, the way we bonded over our love for art. Then she left, taking Angela. I was ten years old and shattered. She never explained why other than to say she and Dad were getting a divorce and some nonsense about me needing stability and Angela too young to stay with Dad. I already told you this. But I didn't tell you the rest. Even though it was hard, Dad and I got along fine. He never spoke of Marlene or Angela. I buried my pain and never let him see. She sent me letters, but I never opened them. I sent them back. She was the first in a long litany of being abandoned.

"At eleven, I watched from my front porch as my little Yorkie chased a rabbit across the street and got killed. I buried him in the backyard. Dad didn't even blink an eye. 'Life and death happen, Destiny. Get used to it.'

"I added one more to my list of abandonments.

"When I was thirteen, I got my first boyfriend, Jamie. He was two years older than me, a freshman in high school to my seventh grade. Looking back, it's clear that it was first-love infatuation, but it didn't feel like it at the time. Jamie was my first kiss. With nothing more than a shrug, he quickly moved on to another high school student. It devastated me."

Enrique gave a wry smile but kept silent and let her talk.

"I know," said Destiny. "To anyone else, it would be chalked up to usual teenage drama. And, more than likely, it was. But for me, it was another check mark.

"When I was sixteen, I had a close girlfriend, Anna, my first real friend since we moved around so much. She meant everything to me. She was my confidante, my soulmate, the female bonding I so badly missed from my mother or my sister. But then she betrayed me, spilling my most secret thoughts to a clique of the popular girls who ridiculed and humiliated me in front of everyone. I was crushed and confronted Anna. She blew me off. Said she didn't need a cry-baby like me for a friend. I was alone … again. Check."

Destiny stopped and gulped from her water bottle before she continued.

"The next nightmare was Dad's heart attack in 2005. I was turning eighteen. My father had been my world, my only face-to-face connection. He taught me everything about life. He gave me the sex talk. We shared every day. I stepped into the role of homemaker at a young age. I cooked the meals, did the laundry, kept the house spit-polish clean. He was strict, believing honor, truth and duty were the pillars of life. He spoke to me like an adult, even when maturity had hardly caught up with me."

Enrique raised an eyebrow in response.

"Okay, it still hasn't. Despite his rigid appearance, I never doubted he loved me. Nor did I dream he would ever leave me so suddenly. The call came from his secretary. He'd suffered a serious heart attack. I dropped the phone. Rushed to the hospital. But it was already too late. He was gone. I was completely alone. Marlene and thirteen-year-old Angela came for the funeral, but to me, it was all a blur. The flag draped over his coffin, the twenty-one-gun salute, the burial at Arlington Cemetery. Marlene offered little comfort, or perhaps I simply rejected it.

"Six months later, I enlisted in the Army. It was all I knew."

She looked at Enrique and clasped his hand. "Then there was Max."

Twenty One

"Army life suited me. The order, the routine, the honor, truth, and duty my father had felt so strongly about. It all made sense to me. As a female in a predominately male world, the military had its challenges, but I held my ground. I did my officer's training at West Point, like Dad, thanks to his position and a reference from Senator Morgan from North Carolina. I worked hard and graduated in the top ten percent of my class.

"I graduated from West Point in 2009 and my first command was as a Second Lieutenant Civil Affairs Officer in Fort Lewis, Washington. It was a plush assignment by military standards, nestled between Puget Sound and the Cascade Mountains. I could see Mt. Rainier from my three-story town-home. But it was so far removed from normal military life, it didn't even feel real."

Destiny leaned back, watching Enrique's reaction. His eyes met hers, but he didn't speak. *This is the easy part.*

"It was a lot of house for one single girl. I spent the next three years teaching civil affairs to enlisted soldiers. The Civil Affairs was responsible for being a liaison between the Army and the civilians in whatever city or country these young men and women were to be deployed. I was a good teacher, and although I loved my students, secretly, I itched for overseas assignment.

"Thanks to President Obama, I got my first overseas assignment to COP – that's a Combat Outpost in Syria—in October 2015 to combat ISIS. It was the exact opposite of Fort Lewis. My job was to make strategic and tactical civil affairs with the Syrian, but they were hesitant to accept an American female soldier."

Destiny paused from her story and went to the kitchen to grab two more bottles of water. She leaned against the kitchen counter, taking deep breaths. She'd tried so hard to block this scene from her mind. Not that it didn't rear its ugly head time and time again. She could do this. *Spit it out.* Squaring her shoulders, she headed back into the small living room and handed him a bottle.

Enrique accepted the bottle. "You don't have to go on. I can see how upsetting this is."

"No, you asked. Let me finish." Destiny twisted off the cap on her bottle and gulped down about a third of it. "In 2017, I made Captain. Dad would have been proud. The promotion was bittersweet. My next overseas assignment was to Bagram Air Base in Parvãn Province, Afghanistan. It was brutal. The climate varied between summer dust storms and temperatures up to 120 degrees and winters with torrential rains and temperatures down to 15 degrees. And the poverty. So much poverty. You wouldn't believe the conditions the Afghanis lived in."

She glanced at Enrique.

He gave a reassuring nod.

Destiny heaved a big sigh. "I first met Master Sergeant Maximilian Stein at a Civil Affairs meeting in a hut full of dark-skinned Muslim men. His blond hair, buzzed into a tight crewcut, would have been almost pure white if he ever grew it out long enough. He spoke seven languages and was fluent in Farsi, Pashto, Pamir, Arabic and Punjabi. An indispensable asset to the mission of civil relations with the local people and the Afghan soldiers. He was the best negotiator I ever met. Max became my second in command. If I were honest, with his piercing blue eyes and rock-solid build, he intimidated me a little too. Despite his pale features, the Afghans seemed to love him, while they were clearly wary—and often hostile—to me.

Destiny glanced at Enrique, contrasting his dark, coppery skin and penetrating brown eyes to Max's Nordic features. Why was she comparing? She shook her head.

"Max could not only put on the charms for the Sunni men and women. The small boys and I were smitten as well. He always had hard candy that wouldn't melt in his pocket, butterscotch, his favorite. I let my guard down and fancied a future with little blond-haired children and a white picket fence. I dreamed that someday this war would be over, and we'd make a life together."

Destiny closed her eyes, remembering. After a long moment, she started up again. "The Taliban were monstrous fanatics to those mostly rural peasants who scraped by on pennies. The children were especially vulnerable. Sometimes the Taliban demanded ridiculously large sums of money, more than equal to a year's income. If the peasants couldn't pay, the Taliban would take a child for their army in lieu of the funds. Parents had to make the awful choice of which child to surrender. A boy would end up a soldier, a girl would become a child bride or concubine. The situation was intolerable, and the most we could do was try to convince the families to seek refuge with the ANP, the Afghan National Police. Unfortunately, many times they were as bad as the Taliban."

Beads of perspiration dripped into her eyes. Destiny wiped them away with the back of a shaky hand. The clock on the wall ticked. She closed her eyes, the action flashing through her mind again and again as if it were on repeat. Her voice broke as she continued.

"On a sweltering August morning before dawn, Max, myself, and a barrage of American and British soldiers made a caravan of Humvees and M1 Abrams tanks heading for Chariker, the capitol of Parvãn Province. The goal was to do some serious negotiating with the ANP. Max and I were in the lead Humvee. About three klicks — uh, kilometers — from Chariker, the rural landscape morphed into ramshackle villages, and the sun began to peek over the mountains. Two small boys appeared, standing in the middle of the road, their hands held out, begging. Barefoot, with the traditional long tunics over pajama pants, they looked innocent enough.

"Could be a trap," said Max.

"Naïve me smiled back and said, 'Oh, I bet they want some food. Got any butterscotch on you?'

"Max halted the procession. 'Of course. You stay here. I'll talk to them—give them whatever they want.' He climbed down and started speaking softly in Farsi. The kids had moved to within a foot of the hood of the Humvee. They couldn't have been more than eight or nine years old.

"I smiled and waved at them, but when my eyes met theirs, something was off. Their smiles were pasted on, but their fear-filled eyes darted left and right. Fear of Max or something else?

"A rooster crowed seconds before the explosion. The Humvee and two others behind it went airborne. The sound pained my ears, pounded my brain. Then—nothing."

Enrique moved closer and wrapped his free arm around her quaking shoulders, never letting go of her right hand.

"Next thing I knew, an Army medic was leaning over me. I couldn't hear anything. I saw his lips moving, but I couldn't hear his words. Worse than swimming under water. No sound. None. I frantically turned my head left and right, trying to make sense of what happened. Debris, twisted metal and something else—body parts—covered the ground. My left arm and hand were gone. But I felt nothing. I tried to stand. The medic forced me back down.

"Where was Max? I tried to call out for him, but my mouth was full of dirt, sand, and blood. I spotted him. When the medic turned his back and moved on to one of the other soldiers, I dragged myself by my one elbow to Max. For a second, we made eye contact. His eyes said, 'I love you.' Then he was gone."

Destiny stopped to take deep breaths. In, one, two three. Hold, one, two three. Exhale, one, two, three.

"Much later, first at the Army hospital at Bagram, then again later at Walter Reed, they told me what happened. The boys were suicide bombers, with IEDs, improvised explosive devices, strapped to their bodies. Children, they were only children. Max was gone. And I couldn't even leave the hospital in Afghanistan in time to see him buried at Arlington."

Twenty Two

Enrique squeezed her hand. "That's rough. You are a strong, brave woman, soldier girl."

"I hardly feel strong, not anymore. Adjusting to civilian life has been hard." Destiny pulled her hand away and wrapped it around her prosthetic. "I don't know who I am, or where I belong."

"Maybe you belong here with me?"

Destiny shook her head. "Your turn. What happened to you?"

Enrique sighed heavily. "Are you sure you want this now?"

"Now or never."

He nodded. "It was December 2001. I had been a hot shot football—er—soccer player to you—in high school." He flashed a smile at Destiny. "I'd been accepted on the Buenos Aires First Division teams. I thought I had an unbelievable athletic career ahead of me. But there was a lot of unrest in Argentina. The government had changed hands several times over a couple years. When the Corralito policies imposed by the latest government restricted people from taking money from the banks, there was an uprising. All hell broke loose. They called it the Argentinazo.

There was rioting all over Argentina. My parents tried to get their money from the banks but failed. Manuel, my brother, was furious. He joined the protestors in the streets of Buenos Aires."

Enrique got up and paced the room. "I tried to stop him. I followed him downtown. He was twenty-one, hot-headed, and thought he could make a difference. He was a fool. It was chaos. The protestors were no match for the heavily armed military. Manuel had a baseball bat. What did he think he could do with that? He smashed the windows of a police car, then turned on a soldier. I tried to get to him to stop. It was hard to see through the tear gas and the smoke and the hundreds of angry people. But they shot him. Point blank. I watched him go down and struggled through the crowd. He was still alive but barely. Pressing my hand on his chest wound trying to stop the bleeding, I screamed for someone to help him. A soldier tried to shove me away, but I wasn't leaving Manuel. I picked up his baseball bat as a deterrent. A butt of a rifle slammed into the side of my head. Then the soldier picked up the bat and started beating me. I could hear the crack of bones breaking in my legs as I held on to Manuel. Then everything went blank."

Destiny moved toward him and wrapped her arms around him. "Oh, Enrique. I am so sorry. They did that to you? Mangled your legs and killed your brother? How awful. How did it end?"

Enrique snorted. "Not well. Thirty-nine people were killed, about half of them minors. The police and security forces faced no repercussions. My parents wanted me out of the country. They said it was for my safety, but I believe they knew I would retaliate for my brother's death. Most of their money was gone, and after 9/11 in the U.S. only three months before, air travel all over the world was non-existent. They had friends that smuggled me into Brazil, then into Cuba. I couldn't walk, and these amazing people carried me. I came with a group of other refugees in a small boat to Miami. I sought asylum here and got my citizenship several years later."

"Have you been back to Argentina? What about your parents?"

"No, I had several surgeries before I could walk again. By the time the borders reopened, both my parents were dead. I have nothing to go back there for." He lifted Destiny's chin and brushed his lips across hers. "So, it's just me. As damaged as you."

Destiny leaned her head against his rock-hard chest. Could she let this man into her life?

Twenty Three

The next morning, Destiny stood and stretched before folding up the pull-out sleeper sofa. The wire frame with thin mattress was far from optimal for a good night's sleep. She recalled the lovely queen size bed in a beautiful room at the hotel overlooking the beach. She shook her head, clearing her mind. *Stop the crap, soldier. Sure beats a foxhole in the middle of a desert or a riot in Argentina.*

Remembering her conversation with Enrique the day, Destiny felt uneasy. Had she made a big mistake opening up and being frank with him? Was she setting herself up for another heartbreak?

Her phone vibrated across the table. The caller ID identified Noah Smithfield from the First American Bank of Marco.

"Good morning, Miss Osgood. We received the tape from the Publix ATM where the funds were withdrawn from your mother's account. Could you come down and look at the tape? If we can make identification, you could press charges."

"Yes, of course. I'm not sure I'll be of much help. I don't know anyone around here. But I can be there around ten this morning, after Marlene's home health aide arrives."

"Wonderful, I'll see you then."

Checking her watch, 8:15 a.m., she peeked in on Marlene, who was still sound asleep. Destiny hurried into the small bathroom for a quick shampoo and shower. Dressing in khakis and a white cotton button-down shirt, she tugged the long sleeve over her prosthetic, exposing only the mechanical hand. She needed to get some more Florida-looking clothes if she was going to stay much longer.

A rustling noise from the bedroom sent her in to find Marlene sitting up in bed. The bewildered look on her face answered Destiny's unasked question of how she was doing today. "Good morning, … Mom," Destiny said. *Mom* still didn't flow easily from her lips, but she was trying. "Ready for breakfast?"

Marlene's mouth dropped open forming a perfect O, but she didn't answer. She pulled the covers tighter across her chest.

By now Destiny knew not to let this rattle her. She went to the closet and pulled out a fuchsia knit top and black elastic-waist pants. Then she crossed the small room to the dresser and pulled out some underwear and a wireless bra. "How about I help you get cleaned up and then dressed?" She cautiously approached the bed.

Marlene stared at the clothes in Destiny's hand, then at Destiny's face. "Are you my helper?"

Destiny felt a stab to her heart that her mother didn't recognize her but offered a smile and a nod.

"That's right. Let's get you dressed, then have some breakfast."

Marlene let her help her out of the bed and into the bathroom. Destiny had never attempted to get Marlene in the bathtub before and wasn't up to it today. After Marlene used the toilet, Destiny sat her down on the toilet lid, removed Marlene's night gown and washed her up with a warm washcloth. "You used to call this a kitty bath. Do you remember that? I'd sit on the counter with my feet in the sink, and you would wash me."

For a second, recognition dawned in Marlene's eyes. "A kitty bath. Yes, I gave my children kitty baths sometimes. Your mother gave them to you too? How nice."

Enrique was coming through the door about the time Destiny settled Marlene at the dining table with a cup of tea. "Well, good morning, Miss Marlene." His eyes, with an additional sparkle, went next to Destiny. "And you too, Miss Destiny."

Destiny couldn't stop the smirk spreading across her face. She knew that he knew she didn't like being called *Miss*. He did it on purpose, to egg her on. "Same to you MISTER Enrique. Marlene is washed and dressed. She's ready for you."

Enrique sat next to Marlene at the kitchen table. "What are you up to these days, Miss Marlene?"

Marlene sipped her tea in the delicate teacup. No acknowledgement of Enrique's presence.

Destiny filled the coffee pot, scrambled some eggs, poured a glass of orange juice for herself and Enrique."

"No, thanks. I already had breakfast," he said.

"Coffee, then?" She set a mug down in front of him without waiting for an answer. "I need to take a short trip to the bank. Will you be okay if I run out while you are doing Marlene's therapy?"

"Of course. We're used to having alone time, aren't we, Miss Marlene?"

She looked at him blankly and nibbled on a piece of toast.

Destiny excused herself and headed to the bank to meet Mr. Smithfield. She hardly knew anyone on the island. What were the chances she would know this thief on the video? Her mind immediately went to Philip. She'd Googled the Collier County arrest records, and her suspicions had been correct. He'd been arrested for grand theft auto in 2008 and spent a few years in prison. How could Marlene be so naïve as to fall for this guy?

Noah Smithfield and Natalie Jensen were there to meet her. "Good morning, Miss Osgood," said Smithfield with a genuine smile.

Destiny offered her hand.

Miss Jensen nodded and invited Destiny to follow them into Mr. Smithfield's office.

"I'm sorry this has taken so long," said Smithfield as he booted up his computer. "Of course, the funds missing from your mother's account will be reinstated. And you have every right to press charges against the perpetrator. We'll need to identify with the cameras exactly how many of the withdrawals the culprit made, but you were correct that there are several months' worth."

Destiny expressed her concern. "I arrived a few weeks ago and have rarely left the condo. I doubt I'll be much help. I don't know anyone."

"True," said Miss Jenson. "However, it's likely someone close to your mother if they were able to get a hold of the debit card and had the code. Unless your mother had the number written down some-where." She stopped to frown and shake her head. "We discourage people from doing that, but it does happen."

"Here we go." Mr. Smithfield turned the laptop so Destiny could see.

Destiny gasped. The camera was angled down, above the person's head, but there was no denying the round little body, the bottle blond short hair, the cat's-eye glasses. "Claire."

"Do you know this woman?" asked Miss Jensen.

"Yes." Destiny could hardly believe her eyes. The video rolled in a continuous loop. "That is Claire Johnson, my mother's neighbor. She's the sweetest thing in the world. She's been a true Godsend to me bringing food and watching over Marlene when I have to step out." Destiny shook her head. "I don't understand. Why would she do such a thing? I'm truly in shock." So much for her assumptions about Philip.

Noah Smithfield turned the laptop around and closed it. "It's hard to say. It's impossible to spot a thief through their everyday behavior. They don't run around with *thief* tattooed across their forehead.

Of course, we'll call the police and file a report. And with your identification, it should be an open and shut case. You do want to press charges against her, don't you?"

Destiny stared at the floor, trying to picture this gentle lady being arrested. "I don't know. It's so unbelievable."

Smithfield hesitated before he spoke. "We *could* bring her in without involving the police first if you prefer. If she can repay the funds, it would be you or your mother's decision on whether to press charges."

"Charges," Destiny repeated. "My God, this is surreal. Yes, please. Let's give her a chance to explain before we involve the police. Is that okay?"

Natalie Jensen pinched her lips together, then turned to Noah Smithfield. "I believe that it is the customer's prerogative whether to involve the police."

"Quite right, Miss Jensen. Miss Osgood can have the final say on this." He turned to face Destiny. "I'll give her a call and ask her to come in. She has an account here, so it shouldn't be difficult. Do you want to be present when I speak to her?"

"Um, yes. I think so. I need to hear it right from the horse's mouth, so-to-speak, to believe this at all."

"Okay, then. Shall we see if we can take care of this today?"

Destiny made a call to Enrique. "Can you stay with Marlene a little longer? We have a situation here."

"Yes, of course. She has forgotten all about school. She is fine. Is everything okay?"

"I'll explain when I get home. Thanks." Destiny hung up and sat nervously in the bank lobby. When she saw Claire exit her car and head toward the bank entrance, Destiny was tempted to cancel the whole thing. How could she accuse this sweet old lady of stealing after all the wonderful things she had done for Marlene?

The minute Claire stepped into the lobby and spotted Destiny, she immediately lowered her gaze, guilt written all over her face. Destiny was sure she knew why she was there.

Noah Smithfield approached. "Mrs. Johnson. Thank you for coming in. May we have a little chat?"

Destiny, Ms. Jensen, and a tearful Claire Johnson followed him silently into his office.

"Mrs. Johnson," began Smithfield. "We have some film from an ATM transaction at the Publix grocery store on Barfield. We'd like you to look at it."

"No." Claire shook her head and wiped her eyes with a white embroidered handkerchief.

"Excuse me?" said Ms. Jensen.

"It's me. I don't need to see." Tears coursed down her cheeks. "I'm … I'm sorry. I know I shouldn't have done it." She pulled Marlene's debit card from her purse and set it on the desk.

"But why?" asked Destiny. "Marlene is your friend."

Claire nodded and dabbed at her eyes some more. "I know. I'm so sorry. It was wrong. I didn't know what to do. I was at my wits' end. My medication costs over a $1000 a month. I can't lose my home and live on the streets. But I can't live without my meds either. What was I to do?"

Noah Smithson straightened in his chair "You're in a difficult situation, Mrs. Johnson, but it's still stealing." He nodded toward Destiny. "Miss Osgood or her mother have every right to have you arrested."

At the word "arrested," Claire buried her face in her hands and rocked back and forth. "I'm sorry. I'm sorry."

"Stop," said Destiny. "She's too upset. Claire, look at me."

Claire raised her head and stared back at her with swollen, puffy eyes.

"Do you have any way to pay my mother back?"

Claire shook her head. Her entire body trembled. "No, I don't have anything. Please don't put me in jail."

All eyes trained on Destiny. The only sound in the room was Claire's weeping.

"No," Destiny finally said. "We won't press charges against you. But you need to find a way to pay my mother back. Perhaps your children can help. You'll have to explain all this to them."

Claire shook her head. "Oh, I can't."

"I don't see that you have much choice, Mrs. Johnson," said Miss Jensen, icily. "Miss Osgood is being very forgiving. I'd find some way to pay Mrs. Osgood back if I were you."

"Okay, okay. I'll call my son. This'll break his heart. But I will pay Marlene back. I promise."

Destiny nodded, feeling almost as bad as Claire. "Thank you, Claire. I know this is hard for you, and you wouldn't have done it if you weren't desperate. Your family needs to know your situation. You can't keep hiding it from them … or stealing from my mother."

Back at the condo, Destiny could see things were not going well. She found Marlene in her bedroom, sitting limply in her chair, totally unfocused, and unaware of what was going on around her. Enrique sat at the foot of the bed.

Enrique gave Destiny an nearly indiscernible head shake. "Not great. I couldn't pull her into the present. She thought you were still in the Army. She's very proud of you, you know. How did things go for you?"

Destiny remembered the album they had found when Marlene had wandered off. Had she really been proud of her? She dropped her purse on Marlene's dresser. "Upsetting, to say the least. I'll explain later." She turned to face her mother. "Mmm … Mom … would you like to sit out on the lanai and enjoy this beautiful day?" She motioned to the sunny day beyond the sliding glass door.

Marlene looked up, but the blank stare offered no recognition.

Destiny checked the lock on the sliding glass door and leaving Marlene in her slipper chair by the door, she and Enrique moved quietly into the other room. Lowering her voice to a whisper, she told Enrique about Claire and the missing money.

"Oh, my God. What are you going to do?"

"Nothing, if she pays it back. I like Claire and hope the best for her, but I have a feeling she'll have to sell her place and move in with one of her children if they'll have her. She can't make ends meet with the high cost of her medications and her mortgage payments."

Twenty Four

Destiny stood outside Marlene's bedroom door; an armload of laundry ready to put away. She heard Marlene rummaging around in her room looking for something, talking to someone — or to no one. More often than not, Marlene was in an alternate reality.

Marlene muttered. "I must tell Steven, show him the blood test. What did I do with his number? Would he still live there? How long has it been? Six years, no five. Angela is five. Mistake, such a mistake. I was so lonely. So very lonely. No, no excuse. Oh dear, oh dear. The blood test will tell it all. What will Frank do? Steven needs to know about Angela."

Destiny's hand rested on the doorknob. *Know what?* Blood test? Who is Steven? If Angela was five, Marlene must be in 1996. Should she interrupt Marlene's fantasy excursion or leave her be? She hesitated for a minute before she turned and walked away. This wasn't reality. Who knew if there even was a Steven.

Destiny moved back to the sunny living room and plopped down on the sofa, setting the folded clothes beside her. Her mind was spinning. 1996.

Not a good year. The same year Marlene left, taking Angela. Coincidence? What had she said about a blood test? It was hard to think of anything from that year except *the leaving*. But there was more. A few weeks before, Angela had fallen off her bike. She broke her leg. A bone had poked all the way through her skin. There was lots of blood and screaming. *Angela's, Mom's, and mine.* Dad scooped Angela up in his arms and raced to the car. He didn't wait for an ambulance. Mom, Angela, and Dad sped away, leaving Destiny standing alone in the driveway. No one thought about ten-year-old her. *Like I didn't even exist.*

There had been something about a blood transfusion. Destiny had looked it up in the dictionary because no one would explain it to her. Angela needed that transfusion. When they came home from the hospital, Dad was furious about something. How did this guy Steven play into this?

Someone must have the answer—if this wasn't all a crazy hallucination caused by Marlene's Alzheimer's. Destiny didn't recall Dr. Goldstein ever saying she would hallucinate. Live in the past? Yes. Not know her surroundings? Yes. Not recognize her? Yes. But never hallucinations.

Destiny scrolled through her contacts on her phone. She hadn't spoken to Aunt Carol for years. Mom and Carol were never close as sisters. They lived on opposite sides of the country now, Marlene in Florida and Carol in Idaho. But in 1991, the year Angela was born, they didn't. Marlene and Destiny had moved in with Carol in Tennessee while Frank was on an unaccompanied tour to Saudi Arabia for

Desert Storm. Surely, she would know something. And it was time to let her know about her sister's condition.

The phone rang several times before someone picked up. Destiny didn't recognize the voice. But of course, she wouldn't. It had been too long. "Hello? Aunt Carol? This is Destiny, Marlene's daughter."

There was a pause before the voice answered. "Destiny. My goodness, it's been a long time. How are you? I heard that you …" She let the sentence dangle. "Are you home from … Iraq? Or was it Afghanistan?"

"Afghanistan. And, yes, I've been back a while now. I'm fine. Thank you for asking." She looked down at the prosthetic. *Kind of.* "But I'm calling about my mother."

"O-ka-y." Carol stretched out the word. "Is she all right? I haven't spoken to her in … oh dear, I don't know how long. She's still in Florida, isn't she?"

Destiny's first reaction was to feel agitated that her mother's only sister had not stayed in touch with her. But who was she to judge? Was she any better with Angela, her only sister? "Actually, Aunt Carol. She's not good. She has Alzheimer's and is going downhill fast."

"No, no, dear. That can't be right. Your mother is much too young for that. You must be mistaken. She's always been a bit of a hypochondriac."

The hair raised on the back of Destiny's neck. "It's true. She has what's called early-onset Alzheimer's. I'm with her right now in Florida. I thought you should know. You might want to see her before …

well … before she doesn't know you anymore." *If she even would now.*

Destiny could hear shuffling on the other end of the phone. What was Carol doing? A tea kettle whistled. It sounded like cupboard doors opening and closing. A doorbell. "Aunt Carol? Are you still there?"

"Yes, yes, I'm sorry. That's awful about Marlene. I'll try to call her soon. But I must go now. I have company arriving as we speak."

"Wait," Destiny interrupted. "I want, no, need to ask you something. Do you know anything about a man called Steven that Marlene might have known when we lived with you in Tennessee?"

"Steven. Yes. Steven Humphrey. He had an art gallery where your mother displayed some of her art. A real looker, if I recall, but a little strange. I haven't thought of him in years. Listen, sweetie, I need to go." The phone went dead.

Destiny stared at the phone in her hand. She'd been dismissed. Well, so much for compassion. If Steven was an art dealer, why would he need to know about Angela's blood test? An eerie feeling crept up Destiny's back. The only rational explanation was that this Steven guy was Angela's father.

No, that couldn't be. The idea was ridiculous. Marlene never would have had an affair. This wasn't the Marlene Destiny knew. Wasn't she? Or was there another side of Marlene that Destiny never knew?

"There you are." Marlene ran her finger down the glossy four-by-six photo. The young man in the photo could have been a look-alike for Kevin Costner in his thirties with his blond hair, startling blue eyes, and full lips, so luscious to kiss.

"Oh, Steven. I never meant for you to know. I never meant to intrude in your life." Marlene sucked in a deep breath. "You have a daughter. And she is beautiful. She's five years old now. Everyone always says she looks like me, but I've known all along it's you, not me, she resembles. She has your eyes. But she's hurt. She needs your rare blood. Frank's going to know. And I guess, you will have to as well. If … if I can find you."

Twenty Five

Two weeks later, Enrique walked through the door, head down, no backpack slung over his slumped shoulder.

Destiny looked up at him from the sofa where she was sorting Marlene's junk mail. The sparkle was gone from his eyes. He looked like he'd lost his best friend. "Something wrong?"

He dropped into the space beside her. "Is Marlene asleep?" he whispered.

"Yes, she's sleeping more and more these days, and very lethargic. I wondered if I should call the doctor."

He shook his head. "No need. It's another step in the illness. I've got some bad news." He rubbed his thumb across the back of her hand. "Because Marlene's not responding to my sessions anymore, I've been pulled from her case. No more Home Health aide. They're reassigning me."

Destiny's stomach lurched. "But what will I do with her? I can't handle her alone." She recognized the narcissism the minute she spoke the words. She should be concerned about Marlene's situation, not her own. "Ouch, that was selfish."

"No, not selfish, understandable. With Claire leaving and me next, it must seem overwhelming."

Destiny flopped back against the couch. "Yeah. I've been watching Claire's children hauling things out of her condo for a week. She hasn't even been over to see Marlene. I hate that I ruined that relationship. Mom loves her." Defeated, she watched as he continued to rub his thumb over the back of her hand. She couldn't help but notice the contrast in his large brown hand against her small pale one.

"It's not your fault. You didn't steal the money. Claire will be better off with her children, I'm sure.

"And what does that mean for us? Will I ever see you again?"

A small turn of his mouth was almost a smile. "Do you want to see me again?"

There it was—that spark she was used to seeing in his eyes. "Yes, of course. You've been wonderful with Marlene."

He cocked his head. "Have I been wonderful for *you*?"

She wanted to run her hand through that beautiful head of black hair, but she didn't. "You know you have, but ..." Was he asking for a commitment of some sort? She wasn't ready. Maybe she never would be.

"But what, Destiny?"

"I ... I care for you. You know I do. But I'm a mess. Remember? Damaged goods? I can't."

"You can if you want to. The real question is, do you want to? I hear you. I know you're afraid of being abandoned again. You think if you get close to someone, they'll leave you, and you'll get hurt. But it's too late for that, isn't it? You already feel something for me. I know it's crazy, but I'm falling in love with you. I can't promise that a car won't hit me tomorrow, but I can promise I'll never willingly leave you. I'm asking you for a chance to make a new life, a whole life, with me in it, 24/7."

Destiny got up and paced across the small room. She didn't speak for a long time. The only sound was the soft snoring from the other room. When she turned back to him, tears glistened in her eyes. "It's too fast. I've only known you a couple of weeks. I need time."

Enrique stood and enveloped her in his arms. She could smell his mouthwash. She wanted so badly to taste that peppermint on her lips.

"And I need you now." His lips pressed against her temple and lingered there.

I know. And I want you too. But I can't. I just can't.

When she didn't return the embrace, he dropped his arms. He stood and stared at her for a long time, as if he had more he wanted to say. Instead, he stepped toward the door and reached for the doorknob. He gave a slight shake of his head. "Then it's goodbye for good this time, Destiny." The door slowly closed behind him.

Her body suddenly felt cold without his arms. *And there you go, like I knew you would.* Like everyone does. It was the one thing she could count on. Everybody leaves. What if she was wrong this time? What if he would have stayed? If only she could learn to trust. *If only.*

From the window, Destiny observed three men loading the last of Claire's things into a U-Haul van. Yet another person stepping out of her life. Claire had been a blessing in so many ways. About to turn from the window, Destiny spotted Claire coming across the small patch of lawn.

Destiny opened the door before Claire could even knock. "Hello, Claire." She nodded toward the truck. "Moving day?"

Claire looked down at the clunky orthotic shoes on her feet. "Yes, I'm going to my son's house in Atlanta." She thrust a white envelope toward Destiny. "It's all there. $4,200. My son lent it to me until I sell the condo. Please forgive me. I'm *so* sorry."

Destiny accepted the envelope and wrapped Claire in a hug. "All is forgiven. Want to come in and say goodbye to Marlene? She's going to miss you."

Claire nodded and stepped over the threshold. "Sad to say, she won't for long, I'm afraid. May I go in?" She pointed to the closed bedroom door.

"Of course. You may have to wake her, but she's slept too long already. I'll give you some time alone with her."

Claire quietly opened the bedroom door. "Marlene, it's me, Claire."

Destiny didn't hear the rest of the conversation after Claire shut the door. She moved into the kitchen and poured herself a cup of coffee. She was losing two special people today, Enrique and Claire. Abandoned again. Perhaps Marlene was the lucky one not to realize the changes in her life. Destiny reached with her left hand to wipe away a tear. A millisecond later, the cold rubber of the artificial hand touched her face and she remembered.

Twenty Six

Destiny went through the motions of taking care of Marlene alone for the next month. Watching Marlene's decline left Destiny exhausted. "Painting days" no longer existed. Marlene rarely spoke and never recognized her daughter. When Marlene did speak, she was somewhere in the past. The silence in the house grew deafening. Destiny turned the TV on for noise, then back off again. She tried listening to music on her iPad. Sometimes she found herself wishing for the sights and smells of war, of times and places she could *accomplish* something, *control* things, *impact* situations.

She'd put her work with the Wounded Warrior project on indefinite leave. There was no way she could abandon Marlene now. What a change of perspective. Angela had been right forcing her to come. Whether or not Destiny ever finds out why Marlene left without taking her way, the important thing was that they were together now.

Destiny set a pair of baby blue elastic waist capris and a pull-over t-shirt with big hibiscus flowers across the chest. Marlene looked at Destiny and the clothes she had laid out for her. "I can't wear something like that to school. I'll be the laughing-stock of the whole freshman class."

Apparently, she was in the 1980's now.

"It'll be fine," said Destiny, exhausted from the constantly changes in timelines. How was she to keep up?

Marlene hurled the clothes across the room and lunged at Destiny, screaming. "I said I can't wear that crap." She flung an arm out, catching Destiny clean across her jaw.

For a second, Destiny saw stars. She rubbed at her jaw. "Mom, stop."

Marlene glared at her. "So, are we reversing roles? I'm your mom now? Fine. Then you can wear those damn clothes." She stormed into the bathroom and slammed the door.

Actually, role reversal was exactly what was happening. And Destiny did not like it any better than Marlene did. Destiny sat on the edge of the bed, fighting back tears and exhaustion. How much longer could she do this?

She moved into the kitchen and poured herself a glass of orange juice. Eventually, Marlene appeared dressed in blue jeans and a Florida State sweatshirt. She scrutinized Destiny. "Are you taking me to school today? I don't know you. Daddy wouldn't like me getting in a car with a stranger."

"I'm not a stranger. I'm … We've known each other for months. But you don't have to ride with me if you aren't comfortable. How about we have some breakfast and decide after that. You could always take the bus."

"The cheese?" Marlene scrunched up her nose. "Only the nerds ride the cheese."

Destiny sighed heavily. What else would this day bring?

More times than she could count, Destiny checked her phone for a message from Enrique. Nothing. Was he still in town or assigned somewhere else? She didn't even know where he lived, although his cell number was still on the white board and stored in her contacts. She wanted desperately to call him but never got any further than the first four numbers before she hung up. What was the use? He had made his decision.

When her phone finally did ring, the voice on the other end wasn't the person she wanted.

A pleasant voice asked, "Miss Osgood?"

"Yes? How can I help you?"

"I'm Nancy Whitehouse from Bayside Memory Care on the East trail. Your sister, Angela, put your mother on our waiting list for our facility. I'm calling to say we have a room available for her now. Are you still planning on her staying with us?"

For a brief moment, Destiny was ecstatic at the opportunity to put Marlene behind her, to go home. She was so tired. Just as quickly, she deflated, not feeling at all like the victor. She may have accomplished her mission physically. Someone was going to care for Marlene, and Destiny wouldn't have to do it. But emotionally, the mission itself had failed. She still didn't know why she'd been abandoned, why she was so unlovable, why everyone always left her.

Mrs. Whitehouse, a little too cheerful for Destiny's taste, made it sound like they were sending Marlene on a vacation, not to a memory care unit from which she would never return. Especially considering it meant someone else had died. Death was familiar to Destiny, but the thought of it still twisted her gut.

"Yes, ma'am, that's right. She's declining very rapidly, and it's more and more difficult for me to care for her."

"It would be our pleasure to have her with us. Why don't you come by? We can go over the paperwork, and you can see her room? We try to leave it a blank slate so our residents can put their own touches on it, pictures on the walls, a favorite chair …" She let the sentence dangle. "It helps settle them in and feel at home."

Destiny agreed to be there the next day while a temporary home health aide from Visiting Angels was with Marlene. Angela and Sam had hired the help so Destiny could get a tiny break to go to the store or to breathe in peace. The timing was right considering Marlene's decline, but Destiny felt empty inside. Why wasn't she happy? Wasn't this what she had wanted from the second she'd accepted this mission to care for Marlene? Now Destiny could go back to her little house in South Carolina, go back to teaching art for the Wounded Warriors, continue with her solitary life. It was karma. This time Destiny got to be the one leaving. Why was it so bittersweet?

She looked around the condo. Should she put it up for sale or rent it out? Marlene would not be coming back. Would she or Angela ever want it for a vacation property? Not without a lot of updating. Best to sell it to help with Marlene's long term care costs.

She phoned Angela and explained the situation. Angela agreed to come and help with the move and to clean out the condo. She assured Destiny that she and Sam would handle any financial needs until the condo sold. If there was any long-term care insurance policy, it had never surfaced.

"Thanks, Ange. I'll pick you up on Friday at the Fort Myers airport," Destiny said.

The following day, Destiny headed to meet Nancy Whitehouse at Bayside Memory Care. Although the grounds were meticulous and the long, one-floor building was well-maintained, Destiny had an uneasy feeling as she parked in one of the guest parking spaces.

A friendly voice answered from an intercom after she pressed the buzzer. "Please show us some identification. Hold it up to the camera next to the bell."

Destiny pulled her military ID out of her purse and held it up. The door clicked open. *Feels more like a prison.*

Nancy met her on the other side of the door. It clicked again, and Destiny was locked in. The sound made her flinch. A flashback of standing in a dirty Afghan prison clouded her mind. She had only been in there an hour before a commanding officer got her released, but the memory was seared into her brain forever. Dirt floor, windowless, a straw mat on the floor. Dirty bucket for a toilet. The Afghan police had arrested her when she mistakenly entered a "secured" space in the compound when she first arrived in Kabul. It was an innocent mistake, but she wouldn't have been the first American to spend the rest of her life rotting away in a foreign prison with nothing resembling a trial or hearing. Thank God for Major General Miles who came to her rescue.

"Miss Osgood, are you all right?" Mrs. Whitehouse said.

Her voice snapped Destiny back to the present. Nancy Whitehouse stood before her, a hand on Destiny's right arm, a concerned look behind her black-rimmed bifocals.

Destiny flinched and pulled away from her touch. "Um, yes, I'm sorry. The lock … it—"

"It's okay. No need to explain. Our residents tend to wander away. For their own safety, we must keep the door locked at all times. We take their security very seriously." Her eyes traveled to Destiny's mechanical hand. Her smile wavered a bit. "How about we take a tour? Then, if you are ready, get to the paperwork?"

Destiny looked around the carpeted lobby and down long narrow hallways extending both left and right. Straight ahead, square tables surrounded by four chairs filled an otherwise-empty dining room. Each table had a white tablecloth with a small bud vase of flowers. Mrs. Whitehouse followed Destiny's gaze and took a few steps toward the dining room.

"We're between meals right now, but about half of our guests come down for meals. We encourage interaction and keeping the routine of meals as much as we can."

"Mrs. Whitehouse, I doubt Mar … my mother, will be able to do that. She's barely eating or cognizant anymore."

"Please, call me Nancy. May I call you Destiny? We're all on a first-name basis here."

Destiny nodded, a lump forming in the back of her throat. She followed Nancy down one corridor of residents' rooms. Most doors were open, and the rooms contained a single bed and an armchair with a small dresser and television above it. Some were pleasant with personal touches of photos on the walls, flowers on the sill. Others were bare, and the residents inside those rooms seemed as vacant as their rooms. *Mom would want her slipper chair and her paintings.* She could hardly believe she actually thought of Marlene as "Mom."

Nancy greeted a few people and waved a hand at others as they passed. She didn't introduce Destiny to anyone.

They approached a small reception desk with a dark-skinned woman in a Scooby Doo smock typing on a laptop computer. She looked up and smiled.

"Destiny, this is Martha. She's one of our aides and helps at the reception desk," said Nancy.

Martha stood and extended her hand. It was warm and soft. "Nice to meet you, Destiny."

Nancy and Destiny continued to a small office to the right of the reception desk. A gray metal desk occupied most of the space, with only room for a straight back chair for Destiny to sit. She gladly sat; her knees unpredictably wobbly.

Nancy sat at the small office chair behind the desk. "I understand how difficult this is for you."

Nancy didn't understand anything. If only she knew how Destiny had resented her mother for the last twenty-five years. If only Nancy knew what a terrible daughter Destiny had been. She never even read her mom's letters, never gave her a chance to explain. And now it was too late.

Twenty Seven

Angela was waiting outside of baggage claim when Destiny pulled behind the long string of cars in the pick-up line. She looked better than she had when Destiny had last seen her in South Carolina. The worry lines were gone, and her hair was newly highlighted and healthy.

Destiny threw the car in park and jumped out, using her good arm to heft Angela's bag into the trunk. God, that girl needed to learn to pack lighter.

Angela threw an arm around Destiny. "How are you?" She looked straight into her sister's eyes. What was she hoping to see?

Destiny hugged her back, then released her and climbed into the driver's seat. "I'm okay. Get in. We're holding up the line."

Angela did as she was told. "Okay, I'm in. Go." Then she shot Destiny a concerned look. "Now, truthfully, how are you getting on? Is it as bad as you thought?"

Destiny shot Angela a side glance. "Ange, it's not good. Mom's gone down fast. It's good that Bayside opened up for her, but ..."

"But you care about her now, don't you? I knew you would. She's our mom. Did you ever get a chance to talk to her, about ... you know?"

Destiny shook her head. "I tried a few times, but every time she'd fade away, and the moment would be over. Did she do it on purpose? Maybe she didn't want to talk to me."

"I don't believe that," said Angela. "Why would she have written to you over and over if she didn't want you to know what happened?"

"We don't know because I never read what's in them. I was afraid she was telling me how wonderful California was without me." The last words came out with a croak as she swallowed a golf-ball size lump in her throat. "And now, we'll never know."

Angela reached across and rested her hand on Destiny's arm. "Even if you never hear her say it, I know she loved you. She told me that all the time. You should believe it."

Destiny shrugged and didn't answer.

The following day, Destiny and Angela packed a few bags for Marlene. Together, they picked out the items to be delivered to Bayside. The bedroom slipper chair, all of Marlene's paintings, her favorite tea pot, and a couple of cups and saucers. The photo of Angela's children. There was no reaction from Marlene, who didn't recognize either daughter anymore.

Destiny sat on the sofa and placed the scrapbook of her life on her knees. She still couldn't believe Marlene had documented every moment of her life: high school graduation, West Point acceptance, that graduation, a newspaper article about her deployment overseas. Another page had all about her injury on tour in Afghanistan and another showing her receiving the Defense Distinguished Service Metal. Where did her mother get all of those? Destiny put them in the box with the other things to take to Marlene's new home.

The Bayside transport van arrived. Marlene didn't resist and let the aide move her to a wheelchair, then use the power lift to place her in the van. Angela climbed in beside her, and Destiny followed with her car.

Room 212, the room they moved Marlene into, was indeed bare. Besides the hospital-green walls, there was only the single bed, a compact dresser, and a nightstand. A small TV mounted on the wall. Her personal things wouldn't arrive until the next day.

"Hello, Marlene. I'm Nancy." Mrs. Whitehouse greeted Marlene at the door. "We're going to be fine friends, now, aren't we?"

Destiny gritted her teeth. Whatever was Nancy talking about? She wasn't Marlene's friend. She was her gatekeeper, the one with the keys to this sunny prison.

"Nice to see you again, Mrs. Whitehouse." Angela offered a hand in greeting. "Thank you for keeping our mother on your list. She'll be much safer here."

Destiny watched her sister. Did she not see what Destiny saw? This wasn't a vacation property.

This was where their mother came to die. She caught herself by surprise. *I guess I do care what happens to her. When did that happen?*

Destiny and Angela stayed with Marlene through lunch and sat at one of the four-top tables in the dining room. Marlene remained in her wheelchair, rolled close to the table. The fourth spot was empty. Some of the residents spoke to each other in soft whispers, but for the most part, the lunch was silent and depressing. Marlene ate little, accepting a few mouthfuls of applesauce Angela spooned into her mouth. After, they settled Marlene settled into her bed, and she promptly nodded off to sleep.

"Well, I guess that's it," Destiny said to Angela. "We've done our job." She didn't feel as nonchalant as she sounded. She turned her face away so Angela wouldn't see the tears glistening in her eyes. This was not conduct becoming to an officer.

Angela let the words sit there in the air without a response. "Ready?" she finally said, picking up her huge Gucci bag and throwing it over her shoulder.

Destiny nodded. With one more check on the sleeping Marlene, she quietly shut the door behind her and followed Angela down the carpeted hallway and out of the facility. The click of the door locking behind them rang in her ears, but she kept walking.

Destiny and Angela spent the next several days going through everything in the condo. They made three stacks; keep, donate, trash. There were surprisingly few things to keep. The furniture was okay, clearly updated not too many years ago, but nothing that either of them wanted. It was best if they advertised the condo to sell fully furnished. Except for the few teapots and cups and saucers that had belonged to their grandmother, the dishes, cutlery, and glassware were all inexpensive and had no memories for either of them. They each kept a few cups and saucers and a teapot. The rest could be donated. St. Matthews House or Goodwill would be glad to take them.

Destiny pulled Marlene's art supplies from the bottom dresser drawer. She'd take a few to Marlene. There was always a chance she would paint again, wasn't there? The rest she'd take home. There were never enough supplies for the Wounded Warriors. She would hang on to a few of the Royal and Langnickel short handle acrylic brushes, far more expensive brushes than she'd ever owned. *Brushes for a real artist.*

Angela sorted through the closet, finding clothes best suited for the donate pile. Several shoe boxes filled the top shelf. She pulled down the boxes one at a time and opened them, more out of curiosity than with any intention of keeping any of them. Each box had their mother's infamous Dymo-label: white dress, black pumps, tan sandals, etc. The last box felt heavier than the rest and had no Dymo-label. She pulled it down and set it on the bed. When she opened the box, she gasped. "Destiny, I think you need to see this."

Angela dropped to the floor and pulled the box into her lap. Inside bundles of letters were tied together with a blue ribbon. Destiny's letters, all of them with "Return to Sender" scribbled angrily across the front. Every single one that Marlene had sent since the day she left in 1996.

Destiny stood in the doorway staring down at the pile. She sucked in a breath. "She saved them. I can't believe it." She sat down beside her sister. Why would she do that? The scrapbook of her Army days flashed through her mind.

"Well?" Angela asked. "Don't you think you owe it to her to at least look at the letters now? For twenty-five years, you held this grudge against her. Isn't it time to put that aside?"

Yes, twenty-five years of pain, loneliness, abandonment. But whose fault was that? Marlene's for leaving? Or Destiny's for never giving her mother a chance to explain?

Angela moved the pile with the blue ribbon into Destiny's lap as they switched places on the floor. "I think you need some alone time with Mom." With that, Angela left the room, closing the door.

Destiny stared at the bundle in her lap. Slowly she pulled the ribbon and let it fall away. Dozens and dozens of letters spilled free. Too many to count. She checked the postmarks and started with the oldest date. Her fingers trembled as she opened the first. A tear escaped her eye and dropped on the letter, smearing a few words. She read lots of sentences in which Marlene professed to loving Destiny forever. Lots of *I'm sorrys* with no explanation.

Destiny's tears dried, and she started to feel vindicated. There still was no explanation. Still no reason to forgive her mother. She kept reading until she opened the one right after her father's death in 2005.

November 10, 2005

My darling Destiny,

We did not really talk at your dad's funeral. I know how hard it was on you. I wanted to wrap you in my arms, but I tried to respect your wishes for distance.

I wish I knew what you were planning to do now. I know you feel all grown up, but you are only seventeen, and to me, that feels incredibly young. Angela and I would love to have you come and stay with us. We have a lot of catching up to do.

It is my greatest wish that you would open this letter and not return it unopened. Now that your dad is gone, I have some things to tell you that I could not reveal before. I made a promise to your father not to say any of this while he was alive.

It's easy for me to blame him, and I know how you would feel about that. So, I am not going to. And of course, I am as much to blame. Probably more so. I'm only going to state the facts and leave the blame-placing for you.

The reason I left so abruptly, taking Angela and leaving you, is because I made a terrible mistake. When we were staying with Aunt Carol while Frank was overseas, I let my loneliness get the best of me. I seriously doubt you remember Steven Humphrey, the artist that had my paintings in his gallery. After all, you were only five years old. Steven was sweet and attentive and understood me. I'm not excusing it, but we had a brief affair. By the time I found out I was pregnant with Angela, your father and I were already back home.

I know it was wrong, but I let your father believe that Angela was his. The timing was only a few weeks off, and he never questioned it. But when Angela fell off her bike and had that severe break, she needed a blood transfusion. When neither your dad nor I were a blood-type match, I had no choice but to confess.

Naturally, Frank was very angry about my betrayal and my lying about it for five years. He insisted that I leave and take Angela. He didn't want to see either one of us again. But he also insisted that I leave you, his only biological daughter, with him. He agreed to keep my secret if I left, partially because he didn't want a scandal that could ruin his military and political career. He had his eyes on an eventual seat in the Senate. Angela still does not know the truth. I must speak to her about it, but I have not decided when that will be yet. She is only twelve years old. All of that is no excuse for what I did. I should not have given in. I should not have left you. I should have fought harder for you. I've regretted it every day of my life since then. I never could stand up to your father, and that is nobody's fault but my own.

I don't have a right to ask your forgiveness, but I am. I can't undo the years we were apart, years you needed your mother so much. But I never, not once in all that time, ever stopped loving you. You were in my heart and prayers every single day and still are today.

Please let me know you opened this. Loving you forever.

Mom

Destiny watched the letter float to the floor. Emotions swirled around in her head. Marlene had loved her all along? Dad did this; he tore the family apart? Suddenly Destiny couldn't breathe. It was too much to comprehend.

Angela was only her half-sister. Her suspicions were correct. Did Angela know this? Should she tell her? Was it even true? But why would Mom lie about something like that? Marlene had confessed to having an affair. She wouldn't lie about that, would she? Destiny needed answers. Marlene was clearly not able to tell her.

Destiny dropped her head into her good hand. Aunt Carol could tell her the truth. Surely Marlene's sister knew. The last conversation Destiny had had with Aunt Carol had been short and distant. Had she been hiding the truth? Did she know and not want to talk about it?

A small rap on the door, and Angela opened it. "You okay in here?"

Destiny watched Angela's gaze fall on the letter in her lap. "Did you get some answers?"

Destiny stumbled over her words. "Yes. No." She couldn't hit Angela with this bombshell if she was not one hundred percent sure it was true. She folded the letter and tucked it under her prosthetic. "Maybe. Angela, did Mom ever tell you why she left me?"

Angela eyes narrowed and she sat down on the end of the single bed. She sighed. "I've told you this a dozen times. No. Only that she and Dad had decided to divorce. She never explained why she took me but not you. I asked her many times. She'd get this far away look in her eyes and change the subject." Angela stared out the sliding glass doors to the boats bobbing in the canal. "Once—"

"Once what?" Destiny asked.

"Once, when we came back from Dad's funeral, I thought she was going to tell me something. She started talking about making mistakes in life and never being able to re-do past missteps. I was sure she was talking about leaving you behind, but she didn't say so. But I was only twelve. I didn't know the questions to ask. So, I let it go, and she never brought it up again." Angela's eyes met Destiny's. "Do you know now? Is it in that letter?" She pointed to the letter on the floor between them.

Destiny shook her head. "I'm not sure, but I think Aunt Carol has the answers. It has something to do with when Mom and I lived with her while Dad was on assignment. I'm going to pay her a visit."

Twenty Eight

Destiny wasn't giving Aunt Carol any chance to hang up on her again. Destiny decided to confront her aunt in person. Promising Angela she would only be a day or two, Destiny booked a flight to Idaho. She knew her sister needed to get back to her family in San Diego. But neither sister was ready to leave Marlene alone in the facility. Both knew that made no sense. The facility was the answer to all their problems, the release of their obligations. But it didn't free them from the guilt.

On the seven-hour red-eye flight to Spokane, Washington, Destiny thought of nothing but the years of mother-daughter experiences they'd missed in her lifetime. Should she be blaming her dad for this separation—or Marlene? And whose fault was it after Dad died? That was all on her. She thought of all the Mother's Days she hated so much. When the other kids in school were making Mother's Day cards and talking about special celebrations in their family, how their dads would cook to give their wives a break. But the words "Mother's Day" were never spoken in their home. Mother's Day was exactly like every other day in her house. Like it never existed. But it did. And each year it hurt, a knife cutting right through her heart. Only the anger she nurtured kept her from complete breakdowns. She thought about the birthdays, at eleven and twelve and thirteen when a conspicuously missing mother overshadowed any celebration Dad tried to compensate with. She thought about the Christmases after Marlene left. Seven years with only her and Dad. Seven years of quiet dinners at the Officers' Club instead of festive holiday dinners with a whole family, a family with a mom and a dad and a sister.

Destiny traded airplane wings for rental car wheels in Spokane. She set the GPS for Post Falls, Idaho, a thirty-minute drive east. The scenery was pleasantly different than looking at the palm trees and the waters of the Gulf of Mexico. Great gray mountains blocked the sun rising over the dense national forest in the east. The one thing that totally surprised her was the similarity of topography between this area and Kabul, Afghanistan. Outside of the dusty, dirty, Middle Eastern city, the land was green with valleys and tipped with snow-capped mountains. An ache tugged at her heart when images of Max blurred her vision. She shook her head and gulped down some bottled water to clear her mind. Having this much free time to think was not helpful.

It was almost nine a.m., Idaho time, when her directions led her off the beaten path into a more secluded area with homes spaced far apart, most appearing about twenty years old, with a few newer ones sprinkled in. She pulled the white Ford Taurus into a driveway of crushed stone. The hand-painted numbers on the mailbox read 249, with the letters

"Crowley" above it. That was it. Aunt Carol's home as listed in Marlene's address book. Suddenly it seemed like a bad idea to show up unannounced. What had made her think this was a good idea? Perhaps she should find a hotel and call Aunt Carol from there. *No, she brushed me off too quickly on the phone last time. I can't give her an excuse to do that again.*

Destiny parked and exited the car, ran her hand down her jeans, and practiced a smile. Would Aunt Carol even recognize her? They hadn't seen each other since her father's funeral seventeen years earlier. Destiny climbed the broad wooden stairs to the front porch and pressed the doorbell.

A gray-haired woman she barely recognized opened the door about six inches. "Yes, may I help you?" Apparently, few visitors showed up on her doorstep this far out in the country.

"Um, no. Aunt Carol? It's me, Destiny." She slipped her prosthetic behind her back.

The door opened wider. "Destiny? My God, what are you doing all the way out here?" Then her face dropped. "Your mother. Did she … did Marlene die?"

"No. she's not dead. She's not good but not dead." Destiny shuffled her feet. "May I come in?"

Carol tugged at the pink fuzzy bathrobe wrapped around her plump body. "Of course. How rude of me." She showed Destiny to a cozy living room with pine wood paneling and over-stuffed plaid furniture. "Please, have a seat. Give me a second to throw some clothes on. Would you like something to drink?"She disappeared down a long hallway before Destiny could answer.

Destiny could have used that drink. Especially some coffee. Walking around the large room, she searched for signs of familiarity. Some family photos, sister photos of Marlene and Carol, or old family photos with Destiny's grandparents. There were none. A huge Native American tapestry hung opposite a floor-to-ceiling fireplace built of stacked rocks and a rough-hewn wooden mantle. Two thick candles graced each end of the mantel with several photo frames in between. On closer examination, Destiny noticed the photos were of a moose. A moose! She would have to ask Aunt Carol about that.

Carol swept into the room in an orange velour jumpsuit. "Now, let's get that coffee pot brewing, and you can tell me all about why you're here."

Destiny stifled a laugh. Did these sisters get fashion sense from each other? Angela would be appalled. Destiny followed Carol into the ancient kitchen. The knotty pine walls continued there, graced with avocado green appliances, a step back in time. The theme here was definitely *roosters*. A shelf about a foot-and-a-half from the ceiling circled the entire room where dozens of ceramic roosters perched. A large ceramic rooster cookie jar sat on the counter. A feeling of dread came over Destiny, one she couldn't pinpoint.

Carol motioned for Destiny to take a seat at a Formica table with chrome legs surrounded by four chairs covered in red plastic. Her aunt set a huge mug with, of course, a rooster on it in front of her niece.

Destiny scooped a teaspoon of sugar into her mug of coffee and waited for Carol to cease nervously skirting around the kitchen, wiping the counter, straightening the dish towels. Finally, she settled across the table from Destiny.

Why was Carol acting so nervously? Was she one of those people simply uncomfortable with unannounced guests, or did she have some idea why Destiny was here?

To break the ice, Destiny asked, "What's the story behind the moose photos on the fireplace?"

"Oh, that's Molly." A genuine smile showed perfect white teeth behind Carol's thin lips. "She loves my apple tree and comes down from the hills to have a snack. She's wild, of course, but she comes so often, I feel like she's my pet. She even brought two calves with her one year."

"That's amazing. Aunt Carol, I'm sorry if I upset you by coming unannounced. I didn't think it through as much as I should have. I discovered some very upsetting information, and you were the only one that I think can verify it—or deny it—for me."

Carol avoided looking Destiny in the eyes. Instead, her eyes were everywhere but on Destiny as if she were inventorying the roosters around the room. "I doubt I have any information for you. As you may know, your mother and I have been estranged the last few years."

That was an understatement. According to Angela, Carol and Marlene had not been close for many years. But why? Angela didn't know, and it didn't appear Carol would be forthcoming now, not without some prodding.

Destiny watched her coffee swirl as she spooned in another teaspoon of sugar. "Did something happen between you and Mom when we stayed with you before Angela was born?"

Carol got up and began rearranging things on the counter.

Destiny pulled the letter from her mother out of her bag and set it on the table. "Angela and I were going through things at Mom's condo. We've moved her to an Alzheimer's facility as she isn't cognizant most of the time." She fingered the edge of the tri-folded paper. "Mom had been sending me letters for many years, but I never opened them, only returned them. She saved them all. Angela found them in a shoe box in her closet. Now seemed the time to read them. This one ..." She slid the paper closer to where Carol had been sitting. "This one is a confession of what happened when she was staying here with you. I need to know, is it true?"

Carol eyed the paper as if her fingers would burst into flames if she touched it. "Well, if your mother wrote this, I suppose it's true." She made no attempt to unfold the envelope.

"Please, Aunt Carol. I need you to read this. I need to know whether this is true or not. It affects Angela too. I haven't even told her what's in it yet." Destiny inhaled a deep breath and sat back, prepared to wait her aunt out.

At the top of the hour, a rooster sprang from a cuckoo-clock and crowed in a volume loud enough to break the sound barrier. Destiny jumped, spilling the coffee, and knocking over her chair. She dove under the table, reaching for her side arm, but only a bloody stump remained where her hand and arm should have been. "Bravo down! Bravo down!" Destiny yelled above the screeching rooster. Debris and body parts filled her vision. Max lay on the ground, twisted and broken. She tried to go to him, but it was no use.

Carol jumped back, nearing knocking over her chair as well. "Dezi, Dezi, what's the matter?"

Destiny cowered under the table, shaking uncontrollably. She only required a few seconds to be return to the present. *I'm okay. Not under fire. No danger. No rooster — at least not a real one. No IED strapped to children. No Max. Breathe, simply breathe.* After a few minutes, she crawled out from under the table, still visibly shaken. "I'm ... sorry. The rooster ... um, I didn't mean to scare you."

Carol ran over to the clock and unplugged it, her eyes wide, face pale. "No, Dezi. I'm sorry." She looked up at the roosters that now glared menacingly. "I didn't know."

Destiny lowered her head, wiped the sweat from her brow, and shrugged, "How could you? Even I didn't remember there was a rooster crow before ... before the explosion. PTSD. It happens like this sometimes."

Carol straightened the chairs and patted the seat for Destiny to sit. "Are you okay now?"

Destiny nodded, sucking in air with deep gulps. "May I have some water?"

"Of course, honey." Carol rushed to the sink and filled a glass from the tap. She handed it to Destiny, mopped the spilled coffee, and removed the mug. Slowly, Carol sat down and used the tips of her fingers to open the tri-fold paper that now had a small brown stain in the corner. She laid it on the table and leaned over to read the words.

Destiny watched Carol's face as she read. Was she reading, or only distracting herself from the scene Destiny had made? Were these words all too familiar? Had she helped hide the truth, first from Frank, then Destiny, then Angela?

Carol leaned back in the chair and stared straight ahead.

"Well?" asked Destiny. "Did you know about this?"

She gave a slight nod. "Destiny, your mother made me promise not to tell anyone about Steven. I knew they were more than colleagues. I was angry at her. She had you, a beautiful little five-year-old. She was risking everything by seeing Steven. We argued. I told her it was wrong. She didn't deny it, but she didn't stop either. I didn't know she was pregnant until after she went back home. The timing was so close, she thought Frank would never know."

Destiny finished for her. "But then, five years later, Angela had a bad fall. The blood transfusion exposed it all."

Carol nodded. "I'm sorry. I wanted children so badly, and she … she had you, then got Angela too. I couldn't forgive her for putting me in the middle. But even more, I was jealous beyond belief that she had what I didn't, two beautiful little girls. We barely spoke after that."

"Do you think she really loved me?" A lump the size of an orange lodged in Destiny's throat. Had she been wrong about her mother all along? Was she wrong to believe that her mother had willingly abandoned her? And if so, what did that do to her idea of Dad being the perfect father? Didn't this knock him off his pedestal?

Aunt Carol reached out and patted Destiny's right hand. "Ah, honey. I know she did. More than life itself. It tore her apart to leave you. Your father was a powerful man with a strong personality. She couldn't stand up to him. She did the only thing she could."

Destiny swiped away tears that streaked down her cheeks. "What about this Steven guy—Angela's birth father. Did he ever know?"

Carol shook her head. "I don't know. I think Marlene tried to reach him when Angela needed the blood transfusion, but to the best of my knowledge, she never did."

"Does he still have an art studio in Tennessee where you lived back then?"

Carol shrugged. "I don't think so, or Marlene would have found him. I'm sorry you're only learning this now. I should have told you and Angela."

"It's not your fault. Many people are at fault, but not you. Mom's at fault for not telling us the truth. Dad for splitting up our family. Me for not giving Mom a chance to explain until now." The tears returned in force. "And now, it's too late to let her know I forgive her."

Twenty Nine

Marlene

I awake with a start. Where am I? My heart sinks. Oh yes, Frank made me take Angela and leave. This is a hotel room. I look around at the sparse room. A single bed. Where did Angela sleep? There's hardly room for both of us in this narrow bed. It's a strange room for a hotel: tile floors instead of carpet, black and white landscapes that look familiar, as if I should recognize them. My favorite chair from back home. How did it get here? Surely, I didn't tie it to the roof of my car. Why can't I remember?

Angela. Oh my God. Where is little Angela? I've told her over and over not to go anywhere without me. I look at a closed door. The pounding in my heart starts to settle. The bathroom. She's in the bathroom.

"Angela, honey. Are you okay in there? Need some help from Mommy?" Throwing the covers off, I notice my legs. They don't look like mine. They're old looking and have no muscle tone. Has something happened to me?

The front door opens, and a woman comes in. "Good morning Ms. Marlene. Want some help dressing this morning? Look outside." She raises the blinds. "Isn't it gorgeous out there?"

My heart starts pounding again. "Who are you? How did you get a key to my hotel room? I'm going to call the front office." I look around for a phone but don't see one.

"Now Ms. Marlene, it's little ol' Nellie. I've been helping you for weeks. There's no need to call anyone."

She reaches toward me, and I scream. "Get away. And where is Angela? Have you done something with my daughter?"

Nellie, or whatever her name is, backs away and raises her hands in surrender. "Now, now, Ms. Marlene. Everything is all right. Let's calm down."

The door opens again, and someone else comes in. "Is everything all right in here?"

She's a little taller than I remember, but I breathe a sigh of relief. Angela. Thank God. "Oh, honey. I was so worried. You musn't leave the room without me. Where have you been?"

Angela and Nellie exchange a look I don't understand. I look away, taking in the pretty courtyard through my picture window.

I turn around and look at two women standing in my doorway. "Do I know you?"

Thirty

The flight back to Florida dragged on forever. First, weather delayed the plane so that it arrived two hours late in Spokane. Then a blizzard grounded it, delaying the flight another eight hours. Destiny gave up sitting on the rigid plastic chairs and found a place on the floor, out of the way, but close to the boarding area. She dropped her rucksack and laid against it, using it for a pillow, trying to sleep, with one ear alert to announcements. Instead of sleep, thoughts of Marlene filled her head. How had Destiny let the relationship get so out of control? It was immature and irresponsible for her to continue ignoring her mother's pleas years after Destiny was an adult. She was as much to blame as anyone.

She closed her eyes and saw the little girl sitting on a rock in the park with an easel in front of her, sketching the other children on the playground. Beside her, Mom sat cross-legged in the grass, blond hair blowing in the wind, her easel pointed toward the trees in the distance. She turned to smile at her daughter and ruffle her hair.

The memory warmed Destiny. Then the heat of the moment vanished with the cold recollection of the day she got the news Marlene was leaving, taking Angela, and abandoning Destiny. The stabbing pain of that memory surfaced. Even though she now knew the reason, it didn't lessen the pain of that ten-year-old child.

Destiny gulped down unshed tears and turned on her side, the hard floor digging into her hip bone. The mailbox. She could see that mailbox with the letters inside. Return addresses from Marlene Goodson. More than once she carried those letters into the house and shoved them under her pillow, sometimes for days at a time before she scribbled *Return to Sender* and rammed them back in the mailbox, flipping up the little plastic flag with so much anger, she nearly ripped it right off the mailbox.

Her mind flashed back to Angela's wedding. Now Destiny could see the cat and mouse game she'd played: Mom trying to get her alone to talk while Destiny dodged her every move. Marlene, so pretty in a long blue dress, her hair perfectly coifed in an updo; but her eyes looked pained, not jubilant like she should have been on that joyful day. *I didn't give her even a minute to explain.*

Again, at Dad's funeral, Marlene had tried to comfort her. The vision of her mom stretching out her arms tore out Destiny's insides. Again, she had been the one rebuking Marlene.

So much time wasted. Time was slipping away too fast to make amends.

The call for boarding brought her back to the airport lounge. Relieved to escape her miserable thoughts, Destiny rubbed her damp eyes, got up, and made her way to the gate. But ten minutes after boarding, the captain announced the flight would be delayed until they cleared the runway of more snow. Another forty minutes passed before they were in the air. She never knew how much she appreciated the Florida weather.

Destiny watched the monitor in front of her as it mapped the trip. *I should be going home to South Carolina, not to Florida. To my quiet little life.* Her mind drifted to her work with the wounded warriors at Fort Jackson. *I miss my life there. I felt useful.* But hadn't she been useful taking care of Marlene? Of course, she had. But that was over. Mission accomplished. Marlene was settled in the Alzheimer's unit. She didn't recognize Destiny or Angela most days. Destiny would be heading home soon enough. She still had one more job. Telling Angela about her birth father. And then there was Enrique. Would she ever see him again?

Her mission had changed so much since she'd left South Carolina. The plan had been to get Marlene to explain why she left her so many years ago. Destiny had wanted Marlene to see that forgiveness was not in the cards for her. That Destiny would never forgive her. She had wanted revenge, justice for her abandonment. She had said she wanted honesty but had never given Marlene a chance to offer it. The trip hadn't worked out at all the way she'd planned. As much as she'd wanted her mother to feel the full brunt of Destiny's hatred, she'd found the exact opposite. She couldn't hate Marlene face-to-face. And her mother didn't hate her. No one was more surprised than Destiny that she wanted her mother's love. That she had *always* wanted her love. She wanted her mother. And now that Destiny knew the truth, she wanted more than anything to tell Mom that she understood. That she forgave her. That she loved her. But was it too late?

The plane landed safely in Fort Myers after a turbulent ride from Spokane. From the pick-up area outside of baggage claim, Destiny watched for Angela in the white Taurus rental. She removed her fleece jacket, relishing the warmth in the air. The loading zone filled and emptied with no sign of Angela. She reached for her iPhone to text Angela when her sister pulled in a little too fast and slammed the car in park.

Angela ran around the rear of the car and gave Destiny a quick hug. "Dezi, I'm so sorry. The traffic was crazy, and no one here drives the speed limit. What's with all these old people?"

"Not a problem. I was about to call you." Destiny threw her small bag in the back seat and jumped in the front. "Waiting here sure beats standing in a blizzard in Spokane."

Angela steered the car onto Interstate 75 and headed south and then glanced at Destiny. "So, did you get the answer you wanted?"

"Well, I believe so. Whether it was good or bad news is debatable. It's complicated." She didn't want to get into the whole thing while Angela was cutting in and out of the slower traffic around them. "How's Mom? Is she adjusting to her new place?"

A wrinkle creased her sister's forehead. "I wouldn't know. She's nearly quit talking. Once in a while, I think she knows me, but then it's gone. I don't think she has any idea where she is. She's going backwards in time, becoming more childlike every day. Like aging in reverse. She's fading away fast."

A lump blocked Destiny's throat, preventing her from replying. Why hadn't she read those letters from her mother sooner? Why had she held a grudge so long? What had it proven? What had it helped? Nothing, nothing at all. She turned her head toward the window so Angela wouldn't see the tears trailing down her cheeks.

"Do you want to go straight there to see her?" Angela asked.

Destiny nodded.

Thirty One

Nancy Whitehouse greeted them at the door of the Bayside. "Hello, girls. Marlene's having a good day. She'll be glad to see you."

Girls? Destiny guessed that to Nancy, anyone under the age of seventy was young. At only fifty-five, Marlene positively juvenile, way too young for this place.

Destiny cleared her throat. "Do you think that she will know us?"

"Perhaps. At least for a little while. She's in a different time zone at the moment."

They stepped into room 212. Marlene was almost unrecognizable. Their mother was sitting cross legged on the bed applying make-up very sloppily. Certainly not the meticulous make-up she'd done in the past.

"Hello," Marlene said when they entered her room. "Are you new to the school?"

Destiny mumbled an incoherent hello.

"Yes," said Angela, playing along with whatever Marlene had to say. "I"m Angela and this is Destiny."

Marlene spread a blue streak across her eyelids. "That's super. I love those names. Perhaps I'll name my kids after you some day."

"That would be fun," Destiny said warily. She looked at Angela, then back to Marlene. "We're sisters, five years apart. How old are you?"

"Thirteen." Marlene leaned forward and whispered. "Don't tell anyone. I 'borrowed' this make-up from my mother's case. She has so much, she'll never miss it." She beamed up at them. "What do you think?"

It was atrocious, everything smeared on too thickly and unevenly.

"Hey, Marlene," said Destiny. "I'm almost eighteen. I've got a little more experience with make-up. Want me to fix it for you a little? And Angela's good with hair. She could give you a great new do."

Marlene's eyes lit up. "You'd do that for me? Awesome." She handed the make-up to Destiny.

Destiny went into the bathroom and brought out a warm wet washcloth and a hand towel. "Let me take a little bit of this off, and we'll start over, okay?"

When Destiny finished with Marlene's make-up, Angela found a hairbrush in the bathroom and brushed out her thin, straggly hair. "I'm doing the best I can, but it's possible they have a hair salon here. We could ask Mrs. Whitehouse to make you an appointment."

Marlene frowned. "Do you think they have a … a beauty school right here in the school? Cool?"

"Maybe," said Destiny. She felt so out of her element. How on earth could she continue a conversation with her thirteen-year-old mother?

After a small rap on the door, Nancy Whitehouse entered, followed by a very familiar face.

Enrique.

She spread the door wide. "Today's your lucky day, Marlene. You have another visitor."

"Hello, Ms. Marlene." Enrique's smile broadened to a grin when he saw Destiny and Angela. "And Ms. Destiny and Ms. Angela."

As handsome as ever, Destiny sucked in her breath. He had on stone-washed jeans and an Argentinian UEFA Cup of Champions soccer jersey. His black hair was slicked back and still wet, like he had recently stepped out of the shower. She felt the rise of heat to her face. "Hello, Enrique." Out of the corner of her eye, she saw Marlene frown.

Marlene pointed at Destiny and Angela. "You two, get out! This is my boyfriend, not yours!"

Enrique sat down beside Marlene like he knew exactly what was going on. "That's right, Marlene. I'm your boyfriend. How have you been, my sweet?"

A triumphant smile spread across her lips. "I'm great." She patted her hair and batted her eyelashes at him. "How do you like my make-up and new hairdo? Do I look older?"

Enrique reached for her. "You're as beautiful as ever."

Destiny cleared her throat. "Um, I think it's time for Angela and me to go. It was nice seeing you again, Enrique. Mo … Marlene. We'll come back and visit another time … when you don't have *special* company." She smiled at Enrique.

"Okay," said Marlene. "Thanks for helping me with my hair and make-up. I'll see you around the school."

Angela and Destiny gave a wave and stepped out of the room.

"Wow," Destiny said as soon as they were out of ear shot. "Thirteen?"

"I know. Kind of creepy. And what was Enrique doing here?"

Destiny and Angela followed Nancy to the front door, where she pressed the buzzer to unlock the door. "Come back soon, girls. Every day can be quite different.

They walked to the car, speechless. Their mother's state was more than either of them could talk about right then.

Within another week, they had everything cleared out of the condo. Buyers were already making offers. It would be a quick sale.

"I've got to head home," said Angela.

"I know. Let's go back to see Mom one more time together. Who knows when — or if — we'll get this chance again."

Marlene lay on the narrow bed, a white cotton blanket pulled up to her chin. She was clutching a doll close to her chest and had her thumb in her mouth. Physically she had doubled in age, now looking about the same as the other patients in the facility. She was badly in need of a color for her hair, now two-toned with blond ends and gray roots. But her facial features were child-like with an innocence about her they hadn't seen before.

Marlene pulled her thumb from her mouth, staring at Destiny. "Mommy?" she squeaked in a timid child's voice. She smiled at Nancy.

Nancy Whitehouse ran a hand down Marlene's cheek. "Hi, Marlene. Who do you have here?"

Marlene held up the doll. "This is Suzie. She's my new best friend." She looked over at Destiny and Angela. "Who are those people? Are they your friends?"

"Yes," said Nancy. "Our very special friends, Destiny and Angela."

"Hello," said Marlene. She went back to playing with the doll, totally uninterested in her new visitors.

Destiny and Angela exchanged glances.

With a tilt of her head, Nancy indicated they should follow her into the hall.

"My God," said Destiny when they were out of ear shot of Marlene. "It's like she's three years old." Had all this happened in the few days she'd been gone?

"At least she's happy these days. One of the aides found that doll for her in the left-over bin. She took an instant liking to it."

"She had no idea who we are," said Angela.

"Not surprising, since you wouldn't even have been born yet in the world she is in now. I know it is hard to comprehend, but it's a blessing in many ways.

Some people never go backwards in time. Those are the guests that are the most unhappy and aggressive. Marlene's in a good place right now."

Destiny and Angela exchanged looks. How were they supposed to respond to that? Nodding, they stepped back into Marlene's room. Destiny looked up at Marlene's paintings on the wall, then back down at her mom. The shriveled woman in the bed with her thumb in her mouth was not the same woman who'd painted beautiful landscapes and ran in the sunshine.

Angela approached the bed first and took her mother's hand. "Hey, Mom, how are you? Destiny and I came to see you."

No response. Destiny stood vigil on the other side of the bed. "Hello, Mom." She leaned over the bed and planted a kiss on her cheek. She stayed in Marlene's direct line of vision. Her mother blinked but didn't respond.

Nancy Whitehouse stood in the doorway. "I'll leave the two of you with her. Talk to her like you would at home. Tell her about your day, what's happening with the grandkids. Something may trigger a response with the present."

Angela and Destiny exchanged looks over the bed. What could they say? Things had hardly been "normal" for a long time.

Angela sat on the slipper chair they'd brought from Marlene's bedroom and fingered the photo of her children on the nightstand. "I talked to Morgan, Chloe, and Chelsea this morning. Morgan said to tell Grandma hello. The girls only babbled. I bet they'll start talking real soon, then I'll never be able to shut them up."

Still no reaction from Marlene. The thumb went back into her mouth.

Angela fidgeted and stood. "I think I'll go check what the doctor's reports say. Will you be okay with Mom for a minute?"

Destiny tried to smile. "I don't know. We might run out of here and tear up the town." Her attempt at humor fell flat.

After Angela left the room, Destiny sat on the edge of the bed. She gulped hard several times. Destiny had to get this out, even if her mother didn't understand.

Marlene stared back at Destiny wide-eyed but not seeming to understand who her daughter was.

Destiny stroked her thumb over Marlene's hand. "I don't know if you can understand me, but I need to say this. I read your letters, all of them. I went to see Aunt Carol. She confirmed what you wrote in your letters about what happened in Tennessee." She watched for any response. Marlene's eyes were open, but there was no focus. Destiny couldn't be sure she understood a single word. Reluctant to let go of Marlene with her good hand, Destiny used her mechanical hand to swipe at tears falling uncontrollably down her cheeks. "Anyway, I know now. It wasn't your choice to leave me. It was Dad's. I should have read your letters when you sent them. You poured your heart out, telling me as much truth as you could at the time. I was wrong. I've learned something since I came here. Do you know what that is?"

No response, simply another blank stare into nothingness.

"I learned I love you. That I've *always* loved you. And I forgive you for leaving me. I only wish you could forgive me for giving up on you." Destiny started to pull away when Marlene removed the thumb from her mouth and squeezed her hand, her grip stronger than Destiny thought possible.

Then Marlene looked directly at Destiny, her eyes clear and focused. She gave a slight nod. "I know. I love you, Destiny," she whispered in a raspy voice.

"Mom ... I—" But Marlene's eyes faded, her thumb went back in her mouth, and she was a child again.

Angela stepped back into the room. "The doctor says ..." She stopped when saw the stricken look on Destiny's face.

"Ange, she spoke to me. She knew me!"

Angela walked over to the bed and touched her mother's cheek. "Are you sure?"

Destiny pulled her sister into a one-arm hug. "She said, 'I love you, Destiny' and squeezed my hand. Honest."

Thirty Two

With the condo empty of all personal belongings and a Sale Pending sign already in the window, Angela drove them to the J.W. Marriott hotel on the island.

Destiny admired the beautiful portico. "This is even nicer than the Hilton where I'd checked in when I first arrived but never got to spend a single night." Finally, Destiny could stay there with the beautiful view of the crescent beach. With Mom safely in the Bayside home, there was nothing stopping the sisters from staying a few days, enjoying the amenities of this five-star hotel. They had earned it.

The first thing Destiny noticed the walls of the lobby were graced with originals of Marlene's work. Her mouth dropped open. Pride filled her heart. The images were breathtaking and could compete with the floor-to-ceiling view of the Gulf of Mexico. Angela led her to a bank of elevators that dropped them off on the ninth floor.

"Wow." Destiny examined the elegant room. The décor was modern but still classical tropics. Above each king-sized bed were copies of their mother's art that hung on the first floor.

"I hope you don't mind sharing a room. I could get you a private one if you want." Angela fidgeted with the key card in her hand. She clearly wanted some sister bonding time. "I can't stay long, anyhow. I need to get back to the kids and Sam. He's going a little nuts trying to be mom and dad while also running his practice. Luckily, he has a great partner who's taken on some of the emergency patients."

Destiny turned from the open lanai door toward her sister "Ange, this is perfect. Did you bring a suit? I've got to get down to that beach." Laying on the sand soaking up the sun would be a good place to talk to her about Steven.

Angela flipped open her suitcase and with a grin, held up three triangles of white fabric. "Yep, let's do it."

"That's your suit? My God, Ange. Why don't you just go nude? That can't cover anything." She pulled her own modest, black, full-coverage tank from her rucksack. "Now, *this* is a bathing suit."

"Yeah, if you're Mom's age." Angela laughed and stepped into the bathroom to change.

By the time she returned, Destiny was in her suit with a camouflage army-green opaque long-sleeve beach cover over it.

Angela raised an eyebrow but didn't comment. Her own see-through mesh cover-up did little to hide anything.

Destiny hated to admit it, but Angela looked great. Hadn't she always? Even after three kids, including twins, she still sported a size three and could pass for a runway model. Well, a short one.

Destiny tapped her left arm. "The prosthetic makes people nervous. So, I cover it up." In truth, Destiny was uncomfortable with the stares. Back at Fort Jackson, even at the pool, where there were so many wounded veterans, no one gave it a second glance. But here, on the beach with all these vacationers? Nope. She'd stay covered up.

Destiny noticed pity in her sister's eyes.

"How are you going to go in the water like that?" Angela asked.

"I won't get in farther than my waist. I shouldn't get my prosthetic wet, and I don't want to take it off." That wasn't entirely true, but Angela didn't need to know that. Although corrosive saltwater and grating sand could damage the prosthesis if she didn't clean it well afterwards, it was technically certified water-resistant.

Angela grabbed a towel and her Ray-Bans. "Oh, I forgot about that. It'll still be great to catch some rays and wiggle our toes in the water."

They headed down the elevator, through the lobby, down the boardwalk and out to the sparkling sand. At least a dozen men, young and old, got whiplash taking in Angela's svelte body.

Destiny and Angela dropped their towels close to the water.

For a bit, they sat in silence, taking in the beautiful view of the Gulf of Mexico, following the pelicans as they skimmed over the surface, then shot up, reversed direction, and dove into the water.

Angela laughed. "They're so funny. I'd think they would break their wings they dive so clumsily. I think they're my new favorite bird."

"Which conveniently can't be made into a household pet," chuckled Destiny.

"Touché."

Destiny reached over and took her sister's hand. "We must get better at staying in touch. I'm sorry I gave you such a hard time about Mom and in the process, not being there enough for you."

Angela squeezed her hand back. "It's okay, sis. The important thing is we did the right thing in the end, and we're going to keep our vow to stay in touch much more often."

"Agreed. Hey, don't let me stop you from going in." Destiny gestured with her chin toward the water. "I'm fine right here."

Angela looked at her, then out to the vast ocean. "Well, maybe one little dip." She stripped off the cover-up, exposing more skin than fabric as she tip-toed over the tiny seashells into the surf.

Destiny watched her go, then lay back on her towel, pulling a hat over her face to block the sun. *When she comes out, I'll bring up Steven. I can't keep putting this off. God, I hope this doesn't upset her too much.* She noticed the unconscious shaking of her foot and forced herself to stop. *It'll be fine.*

When next Destiny looked up, Angela was waist deep in the water, tossing a Frisbee back and forth with a bronzed hunk of a man a few yards away. *Don't forget, you're a married woman, sis.* She was about to go wiggle her toes in the water and persuade her sister away from the strange man when a shadow blocked the sun behind her. She turned to see what or who it was.

Thin, scarred legs led to knee-length board shorts. A dark line of hair ran from the waistband up to a broad, bronze chest. She knew those legs, this body. She felt the smile spreading across her lips before she could stop it. Before her eyes made it to the chin, she softly cried, "Enrique!"

Thirty Three

Destiny watched as Enrique's deformed legs walked around her and came to a standstill in front of her. It was the first time she'd seen him without long pants. No amount of trying could wipe the smile off her face. She stared up at him. "What are you doing here?"

"I could be asking you the same thing." He pointed to her towel. "May I?"

She scooted over, and he sat down, legs criss-crossed in front of him. Except for the legs, he was gorgeous. She forced herself to draw her eyes away from his legs and shifted her gaze to the Gulf where Angela was still flirting with strangers. "Angela and I are staying here for a few days. Well, at least I am. Angela needs to get back to San Diego tomorrow. Thanks for going to see Marlene. I was so glad to see you. What do you think about her condition? She freaked me out when she thought she was a teenager, but you jumped right into the scene like it was normal."

"It didn't take more than a few seconds to figure out what was going on. Figured going along with her was the best way to handle it."

Destiny was touched that he took the time to go see Marlene. "That's very thoughtful of you. Do you visit all your old patients after you're done working with them?"

Enrique covered his hand over hers. "Not all of them. But some. Marlene was special to me. And to be honest, I hoped to run into you."

"Really? Why?" She peered into his dark brown eyes. Any woman would give her left arm for such thick and curly lashes. She looked down at her prosthetic. *Well, maybe not that far.* Her heart pounded against her chest.

He turned his body, moved closer to her, touched her cheek. "I told you before. Because I love you, Destiny."

Was it the heat from the Florida sun or his body that caused her to quiver? A million thoughts flashed through her mind in a matter of seconds. Did she want this? Yes? No? Was she ready? She wanted to be. Wouldn't he leave again like everyone else?

"I can practically read your mind," he said softly. "And no, I will not leave you like everyone else."

"But, how could you have —"

He stopped her with a kiss. "I know," he whispered into her ear. "You've been that broken little girl for too long. It's time to trust someone, Destiny. Trust me." He pressed his body against hers, and they lay back on the towel. The scent of him, the taste of his lips, the heat between them made her giddy with pleasure. She melted in his arms.

A shadow passed over them. "Well, well, well. I'll go to hell. If it isn't Mr. Hotty Home Health Aide. Are you seducing my big sister?"

They pulled away to discover Angela looming over them.

Enrique moved away from Destiny, sat up hastily, and pulled Destiny's wrap across his lap. "Angela." His eyes roamed down Angela's practically naked body. "How've you been?"

Angela's eyes twinkled with delight. "Well, obviously not as good as you at the moment."

Destiny watched his expression and frowned at her sister. "Put some clothes on, sis."

Angela shrugged and did as she was told, taking a little too long wriggling the worthless cover-up over her hips. She dropped beside them. "May I join you, or was I interrupting something?"

Of course, she was interrupting.

"Enrique and I were talking about Mom's 'teen days.'" He certainly handled it better that I."

"Have you seen her lately, Enrique? She's moved to her childhood days. It breaks my heart." Angela pulled a bottle of water from the small chest they had brought. She angled it to Destiny, then to Enrique. "Want some. Looks like you two could use some cooling down."

Destiny gritted her teeth. "Us? Really? And what was all that going on out there in the water? Did you forget about that little gold band on your finger?"

Angela looked down at the band and the three-carat solitaire beside it. "No, I've not forgotten.

I know you've got my back, sis, but I'm okay, merely a little harmless play."

Enrique watched the competitive volley between the two sisters, then stood. "Perhaps I should go." He nodded to the condos lining the beach. "I'm staying over there, in the Emerald Beach Condos. Can I take you ladies out to dinner tonight?"

Destiny gave Angela the silent glare. *Don't you dare accept.*

Angela pulled her eyes away from the scarred and disfigured legs and gave an almost indecipherable nod. "I'd love to, but I must decline. I've got to catch an early plane home tomorrow. It's so good to see you again. And thank you for the wonderful job you did with our mother."

"And you, Miss Destiny?"

"That would be lovely, Enrique. I accept. Meet me in the hotel bar?"

"Seven o'clock. It's a date." He leaned down and brushed a kiss across her lips. Then he was gone.

Destiny and Angela watched him walk away across the sand.

"Well, that was certainly interesting. I knew there was something going on between you two. Even if you didn't come out and say it."

Destiny shrugged. "I can't exactly say anything happened before. A few kisses." She sighed and stared out at the ocean. "Am I crazy to be falling for him? What kind of future would we have? A home health aide that works for Medicaid?"

"Money was never important to you, Dezi. I'm the material girl, not you. And why couldn't it work? If anyone can help you learn to function …" She stopped and motioned to the prosthetic. "He can. And with his experience and own …" —she struggled to find the right word—"disability, he could even be interested in helping out with your Wounded Warriors. You could be a team."

Destiny hated the word *disability*. It made her feel less worthy. Did Enrique feel that way with his injuries? "What makes you think he'd leave Florida for me?"

"Oh, come on, Dezi. That puppy-dog-love-sick look in his eyes says he'll follow you anywhere."

Destiny laid back on her towel and pulled her sun hat over her eyes.

For a few precious moments, Angela sat quietly.

Destiny's mind went back to the letter. *I need to tell her about Steven. Wasn't that my plan when we came down here to the beach? Perhaps it can wait a bit, but definitely before she leaves for San Diego.*

Thirty Four

Destiny watched as Angela scurried around, scooping items she'd left everywhere and stuffing them into her suitcase. With one arm, she swept her side of the bathroom sink clean of multitudes of lotions, make-up, and other personal items, and filled a one-quart zip-lock bag. Destiny's meager one lipstick, a tube of toothpaste, and a toothbrush looked lonely without all of Angela's stuff. Destiny plopped down on one of the king-sized beds and sat crisscrossed. "Are you anxious to get home to Sam and the kids?"

"I am. I bet the kids have grown three inches, and Sam's going to be ready to divorce me if I don't get back soon."

"You've only been gone three weeks. How fast do kids grow?"

Angela leaned her entire body across her suitcase to get it to close. "So, I exaggerate a little." It snapped shut with a triumphant click. "But I'll miss you. Even with everything happening with Mom, it was great spending time together. You've got to promise we won't stay apart this long ever again."

"I imagine we'll both be back and forth here for a while, looking in on Mom." They both knew that more than likely they would be coming and going, taking turns rather than being in Florida together. "You can always come to South Carolina to see me. Bring Sam and the kids. Take a little vacay."

Angela nodded unenthusiastically.

Was her sister thinking the same thing as Destiny? Would the next time they got together be for Marlene's funeral? Destiny didn't want to think about that.

"Ange, there's something I need to talk to you about." Destiny reached for the bottle of wine on the desk. Pouring them each a half glass of Pinot Noir, she handed a glass to Angela.

Angela accepted the glass and raised it in a toast. "To Mom."

"To Mom." Destiny twirled the stem of her glass. "When I went to see Aunt Carol, she told me something I need to share with you." When Angela didn't respond, she continued. "Mom and I were staying with Aunt Carol while Dad was overseas, and she, meaning Mom, got involved with another man. I don't blame her exactly; it's hard to be a military wife. But shortly after Dad came stateside and we got back together as a family, she realized she was pregnant."

Destiny watched her sister. She sat there, sipping her wine as if she didn't have a care in the world. Was she not getting the connection? "The timing was so close that the baby could have been her lover's—or Dad's."

Still nothing from Angela.

"Ange. *You* were that baby. Remember when you fell off your bike and broke your leg so badly you needed a blood transfusion?"

Angela raised her hand in the universal sign to stop. "It's okay, Dezi. I figured it out. Well, with some help from my doctor. When the kids were born, my rare blood type came to his attention. We checked to see if Mom or Dad had it. Neither did, but the DNA proved I belonged to Mom, but not to Dad. I figured out that's why he didn't want anything to do with me. I wasn't his child."

Destiny fell back against the pillow as if she'd been knocked out by a punch. "Wow. Did Mom ever 'fess up to you? Tell you who your father is?"

Angela nodded sheepishly. "Yes. I confronted her after Morgan was born. I figured that was what was in the letters to you."

Destiny looked aghast. "You lied to me. You said you didn't know. Why?"

Angela held up a hand. "I know. Sorry. She told me that the truth had to come from her and swore me to secrecy. Besides, who my father is, or was, is *my* story. Not yours. And I couldn't tell you that part without telling you why Mom left and took me and not you. Dad"—she did air quotes—"didn't want any part of his bastard child." She wiped an unexpected tear that smudged her perfect make-up. "You see, I had the same abandonment issues as you—you might say even worse—as I've been rejected by two fathers."

Destiny dropped her head into her hand. "Oh, God. Did you meet Steven?"

Angela shook her head. "Mom said that she tried to reach him after my fall and broken leg. But she couldn't find him. Then I tried myself after Morgan was born. That's why I wanted you to read Mom's letters."

"Did you know she had been keeping them all along?"

"No, I was so excited to find them. I had no idea she'd kept them. But I was sure the confession was in there after Dad's death. But you had to find it out for yourself. What was between you and Mom had to stay between you and Mom. And what *isn't* between me and my birth father, never will be. I am a fatherless child."

Destiny crossed the short distance between their beds and wrapped her arms around her sister. "Oh, Ange, I'm so sorry. You must think I've been a horrible sister."

The corners of Angela's lips curled up. "Perhaps sometimes. But you know now. You know that Mom always loved you. She wanted to be with you more than anything. I'm so glad you got a miniscule moment of reality with her when she told you.

"Me, too. Think of all the years I wasted not enjoying having a mom."

"Well, you can't change that now. Shouldn't you be getting ready for your big date with Mr. Hottie Lopez? I'm going to take a long, hot bath and call it a night. I'm leaving for the airport at four a.m. You'll be sound asleep when I leave unless you don't come in at all." A twinkle sparkled in her eyes.

"I'll be back way before that, and you had better wake me up to say good-bye."

Angela headed into the bathroom and shut the door.

Destiny stood at the small closet staring at her one dress and three shirts. She didn't have anything exciting to wear. She pulled the dress off the hanger and laid it on the bed. A simple cotton, sleeveless knit. At least it hugged her body nicely. With her favorite scarf to wrap around her shoulders and across her prosthetic, she was as good as she was going to get. She slipped it on and stared at herself in the mirror. Certainly not the beauty of Angela. She wrapped on the bathroom door. "I'm going down to meet Enrique in the bar. Wake me up before you leave. Promise?"

"I promise. Now go have a fabulous time."

The bar was nearly empty. The white-washed wainscotting with nautical paraphernalia gave her the feeling of standing in a large cabin on a yacht. And there, center stage hanging above the bar, was a large painting. It had to be six feet square. Destiny recognized her mother's style immediately. The image depicted a porthole of a ship looking out to a vast sea of foaming waves and an endless horizon. A school of dolphin danced far out at sea. Destiny moved toward it and took a seat at the bar.

The bartender saw her staring at the painting. "Pretty amazing, isn't it?"

"Yes, it is."

He turned and stared at it too. "I always feel like I'm out at sea, traveling the world when I work here."

"My mother painted that."

The bartender turned back to her. "Seriously? Wow. That's awesome. Does she still paint? I'd love to meet her someday."

The smile slipped from Destiny's face. "I'm afraid that isn't going to happen. She's in an Alzheimer's unit in a nursing home. I don't think she'll be coming out again."

The bartender made an indecipherable sound from the back of his throat and busied himself wiping the counter. After a few seconds, he looked up. "May I get you something to drink?"

"Make that two Mojitos, one for the lady and one for myself." Enrique sat beside her.

Destiny turned in surprise. "Hey, you snuck up on me."

"You were captivated by Marlene's painting. Everyone's astounded by its beauty."

She turned and admired the porthole again. "Yes."

The server set their drinks in front of them and made his way to the other end of the bar.

Destiny and Enrique sipped at their drinks, saying little. When they were done, Enrique paid the tab and ushered her out the door. "We have reservations at Salé Pépé's. Have you been there before?"

Destiny laughed. "Well, of course. I have all my suitors take me to a different five-star restaurant every night. Don't you know?"

"Is that so? Well, I'd better tell them your calling card is booked. Forever. I hope I'll be the last suitor taking you anywhere."

They walked hand-in-hand the two blocks to the Marco Beach Ocean Resort and took the elevator to Salé Pépé's. Enrique had reserved a table for them on the lanai overlooking the beach. Everything was impeccable, from the server in his starched tuxedo, to the beautiful table setting, and of course, the view. It made the idea of living in land-locked Columbia, South Carolina, feel very confined. Something about endless views that crested the horizon made Destiny feel insignificant among the vastness, and at the same time, somehow connected to the earth in a way she'd never felt before.

Enrique ordered for them. They sipped a cocktail while waiting for their dinner. He clasped her hand. "When are you leaving?"

"I have reservations for tomorrow. Non-stop from Fort Myers at six p.m. I'll need to be there by four."

He squeezed her hand a little tighter. "I want to go with you, Destiny. Let's start our life together. Don't those soldiers of yours need home health aides as well as art therapists? We could make this work between us. I know it."

Destiny remembered Angela's words. She considered the beautiful view, then turned to him. "You'd leave all this for me?" She nodded at the water. "It's not nearly as beautiful there."

"Everywhere is beautiful if you're in it."

She groaned.

He raised an eyebrow. "Too corny? But I mean it. I love you, Destiny. I won't push you. We can take it slow. I'll even get my own place. Give us a chance."

Destiny leaned in and kissed him. "I love you, too." She kissed him again. "But I'm not ready. I'm sorry. I'm still such as mess. I'm afraid I'm going to be a long, slow project. "Healing this" — she touched her temple — "may be a slow process."

Enrique's grin said it all. "I'm not happy about it, but I'll wait as long as I have to."

Thirty Five

It was good to be back in her little bungalow. Thank God she'd found someone to keep it dusted and mopped while she was gone. It smelled wonderful. Destiny plopped down on the sofa and breathed it all in.

After unpacking, her first call was to Master Sergeant Clemmons at Fort Jackson. "Hey, Sarge, I'm back. Still have room for me as an art therapist? I'd totally understand if you don't need me anymore."

"Are you kidding me? We can't wait to have you back. Have you ever seen me try to draw anything? The soldiers keep asking about you. Ready to start Monday?"

A warm feeling filled her heart. "Yes, sir. I'll be there at zero 800."

Days turned into weeks. Destiny and Angela Facetimed daily, even if it was only for a few minutes. Destiny surprised herself about how much she was feeling toward her niece and nephews. She never thought children would ever be an option for her. But now, who knew what the future would bring?

Her cell phone rang. Destiny recognized the rehab facility.

"Destiny? This is Nancy Whitehouse. I am so sorry to tell you that your mother passed away this morning."

"Oh," said Destiny. Of course, she knew this was going to happen, but the reality of it was a kick to the gut. "Um, I'm sorry. I don't know what I am supposed to say."

"Understood," said Nancy. "We're transporting her body to the morgue. The funeral home can pick it up from there. Do you have one in mind?"

Funeral home. Why hadn't she and Angela discussed this. "Umm. I don't know. Let me talk to my sister. We'll come right down. Do you need to know today?"

Nancy Whitehouse's voice was soothing and calm. An unfortunate part of her job. "No, let the Collier County morgue know as soon as you make a decision. There's a lovely funeral home on Marco Island, and it's right around the corner from the Marco Island Cemetery, unless you have a plot somewhere else.

Destiny hung up the phone and sat in stunned silence. Her next call was to Angela.

Angela and Destiny's flights both landed in Fort Myers within an hour of each other. There were no words to comfort each other. Amazingly to Destiny, Angela had taken total control of all the decisions, seamlessly and efficiently. Destiny acquiesced to all her suggestions.

The decision was for a cremation and burial of the urn at the Marco Island Cemetery after a small gathering at the funeral home on Marco for Marlene's friends to say their goodbyes.

The condo had been sold, and the sisters again booked a single room at the JW Marriott.

"What did you bring to wear," asked Destiny as she unpacked the few belongings; a black sleeveless dress with a chartreuse wrap to cover her prosthetic, a few pairs of shorts and T's and enough undies for a weekend.

Angela held up a black and white polka dot swing dress. "I couldn't deal with all black. I hope it's okay."

Destiny smiled at her sister. "Anything short of cut-offs and flip-flops would be fine. Things are much more casual down here. I wonder how many people will show up today?"

"Are you expecting Enrique?" Angela asked with a raised eyebrow. "I did post a notice in the local newspaper. Have you heard from him?"

Destiny shook her head. "A few texts when I first got back to North Carolina, but I wasn't ready to deal with him. I didn't respond."

Angela frowned. "You have a bad habit of ignoring correspondence. Don't do to Enrique what you did to Mom. If he shows up here, talk to him. I know you still have feelings for him."

"I do," said Destiny. "I've tried not to, but the absence only makes my heart want him more. I didn't think that theory was real. But it is. I think I want him more now than ever."

"And are you ready to let him know that?"

"We'll see."

Destiny spotted Enrique the second he stepped through the door of the funeral home. Dressed in black dress pants and a black button-down shirt, he was everything she dreamed about.

Enrique patiently stood in reception line through the dozens of bottle-blond ladies and gray-haired men. At the front, he ran his hand gently over the urn and admired the photo of Marlene beside two of her favorite paintings. Finally, he reached, first Angela, then Destiny. He kissed them both on the cheek, but he lingered with his hand clasped firmly in Destiny's. "Hi, babe. So sorry for your loss."

Fresh tears sprang to Destiny's eyes. "Hi to you too. Thanks for coming."

Enrique leaned over and whispered in her ear. "When this is all over, may I have a little alone time with you? Please?

"Yes, I'd like that," she said through her tears.

Destiny and Enrique sat together on a cement bench at the Marco Island Cemetery long after everyone else had departed and Angela had gone back to the hotel.

"I've missed you so much," said Enrique. "You didn't respond to my texts. I finally gave up. If you wanted me, you'd have to find me."

Destiny offered a weak smile. "Yeah, I'm bad at that. You'd think I would have learned. I'm still working through some issues."

She turned and leaned into him. "I'm ready now, if you still want me. You've taught me so much. I'm going to have to change my mantra."

"To what?"

"Everybody DOESN'T leave."

Joanne Simon Tailele

Alzheimer's

by Don Erdek
1935-2020

The dawn fades as life's sunset appears.
No flags, no signs, no thresholds to guide.
With stealth, with age, with a shadowy cloak
the dotage darkens.

Alzheimer's invades without a sound.
So quiet it steals the memory.
I don't remember that event.
I can't recall that predicament.

The senses dull in non-response.
The passion now lost; no longer to find.
Emotions slack and slaked by time.

Why remember if there is no need.
Why retain an experience, a happening,
a thought, if it is of no use.
Old memories like old clothes simply don't fit.

Alzheimer's a loss of memory or a loss of a
need to remember.

For you see it is more than a closet of old clothes
that don't fit.
It is the "it" in the "fit" that fits no more.
That move to self-darkness of not knowing me.

It is the "it" that sees not the aging me.
The "it" senses not the onset of senility.
The "it" accepts this siege without a whimper,
without a fight.

"It" knows of staggering steps, the loss of sight.
"It" senses the quaking hand, the strain to hear.
But the "it" shies away from the worst to fear
 - the loss of who I am.

Anxiety may precede the loss of knowing.
Horror of not knowing when the who I am no longer knows.
A burden to not know who I am but more so for
them that know.

A tragedy for family.
A pity to friends.
A total unawareness most likely for me.

Dread and sorrow, a failure to cope,
ensnares those others.
The me to be oblivious of the darkness
descending on me.
My heart, my breath will strain for survival.
My departing mind gives not a clue that the body
no longer has a thoughtful thing to do.

248

249